BROTHER'S KEEPER, SISTER'S CHILD

For Clyde and James

IT BEGAN FOR MAE with a letter she never sent.

If she had finished the letter and mailed it on to Danny, perhaps he would have stayed with her at Thanksgiving and nothing would have happened. If she had never begun the letter in the first place, never, that is, listened to the vague insistent voices which urged her to write him, possibly nothing would have happened, anyway, and certainly she would not have been left, as she was in the end, haunted by her sense of having failed to meet a responsibility.

She woke up that morning with anxiety cramping her stomach as it had at the conservatory towards the end of every semester as recitals loomed closer. She hadn't needed her teachers then to remind her that she wasn't ready to get up on stage. But the quartet's concert last night had gone off well. They had never played that final movement of the Beethoven better. Andy's double stops had been perfectly in tune. The audience had clapped them back on stage for a third bow, and when they'd rushed off the last time, Andy pulled the four of them into a tight, exultant embrace. "Yeah, team," he said, pulling Mae's hair. "One more for the Gipper."

Mae's bow arm felt stiff. Reaching her hands over her head, she pointed her toes hard in the other direction, pulled every muscle taut, held her breath, then relaxed. But the uneasiness remained, hovering over her while she showered and patted lotion on her face and scowled into the mirror at the lines on her forehead, a consequence of years of peering at music in poorly-lighted concert halls.

She didn't dress. Friday mornings she reserved for herself. No students, no rehearsals. She usually came in late after a Thursday concert, and, with something big scheduled for the weekend, a recital or restaurant or wedding to play, she wanted solitude. Bookings were just coming in again after the slow summer season. Mae put on her blue kimono, given to her by a former student one Christmas, tying it with an Indian scarf (gift of another student on some other Christmas), as she had promptly, not unexpectedly, lost the original blue sash. With her coffee balanced on the flat arm of her favorite chair, knees hunched up under the robe, she tried to think what it was that was nagging at her. There must be something she was supposed to do that she had forgotten about, though Andy would have reminded her if they'd planned an extra rehearsal for Sunday's cantata. He was used to her forgetting details she preferred to ignore, even though such a rehearsal would bring in a nice fee, union scale.

It couldn't be that she had forgotten to call anyone. Most of her friends were out of town for Labor Day, and she had talked with her sister Justina not two weeks ago. Andy would call later and Max —but she'd as soon not talk to Max. Still, there was something, but she couldn't think what, and held the heavy mug to her chin, admiring the threads of lilac sealed in the glaze, not drinking, just savoring the fragrant steam which warmed her lips. Today was the one morning of the week when she measured time by how long it took to finish her coffee. Nothing broke her morning into increments, nothing outside the cooling coffee and her body curled into the circle of her chair demanded that she move; she need not rise and quickly swallow, rinse her cup and set it in the sink and rush to greet the student ringing at her door. Time, held like the liquid in her cup, was still. This was a weekly indulgence more necessary than sleep to one whose measured minutes were split again into segments beat off by a metronome: so many beats to the measure and the quarter note gets one beat. Time was the rhythm pulsing steady as a foot tap through her brain, pulling her forward through a melody, propelling her through a day.

Except on Friday mornings. She studiously ignored the stereo with its great speakers behind her. The radio with its on-the-hour news clips would only alert her to the passage of time. And music, no matter who the conductor, how fine the orchestra, would switch on that part of her mind that she was now so carefully resting. The part that, listening, analyzed and corrected before she even knew that she was comparing the sounds that she heard to the ideal music which dwelt, after so many years of study, somewhere inside her ear. This sense lay (so she believed) outside her brain; too often it forced her to react before she'd had a chance to think about what she was saying—it was what made her cry out in the middle of a student's lesson when, with any thought, she would have offered her criticism in the gentlest of tones. It was also what made her grimace when Andy hit a false note twice running in rehearsal, when she wouldn't hurt Andy's feelings for the world.

So now she shut her ear to its profession and revelled in the silence. That is, the almost silence of a city apartment where always in the background traffic whispered and there was the whooshing pause-before-take-off of an aging bus. Mae lived high enough above the street that noise was muffled, not-quite-real, a mere hint of the life outside her own.

Her fingers stroked the now-cool coffee mug, tracing uneven spots in the glaze as another woman might caress her child's face. Looking up at her was her own face in miniature, the nose tip-tilted, brown eyes darker in the glossy pool held by the perimeters of lilac pottery. Danny had made it for her at camp one summer, promising her another because she'd liked it so much. It was so complete, her life, so rounded in; it was no wonder she couldn't remember anything outside which she had neglected. She lived within an order which seemed to have attached itself to her ear's need for perfect pitch. Her concert black dresses, long for evening, short for afternoons, were pressed and always ready in the closet. New library books she kept by the bed; trade magazines and lives of the composers she spread on the hall table for her students to read as they waited their turn in the studio. Plants with leaves glossy from weekly washings were arranged across window sills among trinkets from her younger students—special rocks, pot-pourri jars, carved animals. And in her music room (the perfect size for a nursery, her landlady told her) the four music stands stood like tethered horses patiently waiting for the quartet to ar-rive. No one re-arranged the music which was alphabetized along one wall, or questioned the slap-dash order of the photographs hung on another: pictures of friends at music camps and outdoor playing parties mixed with formal poses of their professional post-ers and the stiff unhappy faces of her sister Justina's children caught by school photographers at precisely the most awkward moments. On the back wall, behind the baby grand piano which she rolled into the middle of the room when they did piano quintets, hung a ballet mirror so her students could see what they were doing right or wrong; beside it, the Degas she loved to practice by, intrigued always by the dancers' disciplined but somehow clumsy poses and the indifferent arrogant authority of their dancing master.

Andy, who was divorced after seven years of family life, agreed with her how wonderful it was, this solitude. No one to pick up after, to worry over. "Sure, I bet your sister wants to go back to work full time. She'll have an office to herself," was his only com-ment after Mae had raved to him for two hours about the chaos of the Pearson home. She'd returned from a weekend in Ashe-ville craving their reunion bottle of wine and Andy's calm. "Three children, but you'd think there were a dozen the way Justina falls apart," she told him over the first glass. By the third, she was able to convey to him her sense of being emotionally battered there. "The problem of course is that Daniel's more demanding than all three kids put together. He insists on quiet so he can work, then screams if there's a sound. All through Saturday supper he wouldn't say a word because Danny had invited over a friend without checking first to see if it was convenient. Convenient for Daniel, that means. Daniel would never bother to recall that it's Justina who serves the meals. According to his schedule." She finished her wine. "Sunday we couldn't eat dinner until three because he was in the middle of revising a chapter and wouldn't be interrupted. He came down-stairs all bright and bubbly because he'd finished. The younger kids were grouchy, they were so hungry and Danny was seething be-cause he missed a soccer game." Andy shook his head, laughing a little. "Maybe it sounds funny to *you*," Mae began. "Oh well, it'll probably be calmer down there when Danny goes back to school."

Mae yawned, and pulled herself out of her chair. If she was going to meet Andy at the coffeeshop by noon, she had to start her practicing. Out of long habit she went first to the kitchen to rinse out her mug and wipe the already clean counter top. Compulsively tidy, Andy said. Compulsive, anyway. She couldn't drink her morning coffee out of any mug but this. It wouldn't taste the same.

The click of her mug as she set it on the counter focused her thoughts. Danny. It was something about Danny which had woken her. There was no one else who would tug at the back of her consciousness in quite this way. Danny was her sister's child, but he was her boy.

She'd driven with Justina to his school for the first Parent's Weekend last October. After they'd turned off the highway, the private road had gone on and on, winding through empty fields, then fields fenced in for horses Justina said belonged to the school, then the playing fields, their soccer nets billowing in the wind, then, finally, around a wide flat lawn (how did Danny, brought up in the mountains where the blue of the sky and the deeper dusky blue of the Smokies met and merged, endure such flatness?) to stop before low white buildings grouped around a courtyard. It looked just like a monastery. To the boys on the steps of the Admissions Office, staring at the car as if greedy for anything new and noisy, it probably was a monastery. As she followed Danny and Justina from building to building, picking her way in high heels across the muddy paths on the mandatory tour boys gave their parents ("And this is where we went for our physical the first week"; Justina replying with the expected concern, "And are the doctors here good doctors?"), Mae found it difficult to imagine any sixteen-year-old enduring the isolation long. She supposed (they were touring the new library) it was a good place for studying.

Danny had seemed contented with his new school, though it was difficult to be sure of anything he felt through the mask he assumed when around either of his parents. Mae got a few minutes alone with him in Boston while Justina packed for her trip South. The two of them had walked along the Charles, licking ice cream

cones which Mae had insisted on buying for them in a last effort
to instill a festive spirit into the weekend. A single scull kept pace
with them, then raced ahead along the flat gray water. Mae had
found it difficult, all weekend, to find things to say which seemed
appropriate to his mood and to Justina's, and had settled finally
on a kind of bright breeziness which would leave Danny free to
respond however he liked. As they paused on the footbridge to
look down the river, she found herself regretting her choice of
tone. It was not so easy to break out of it now.

"I've stood on this bridge so many times, wondering about
things," she said. "Before concerts, trying to get psyched up to play;
after concerts, trying to forgive myself for mistakes. I think every
date I've ever had has walked me to this bridge."

Danny had dropped the last of his ice cream cone into the river
and was leaning on his arms, watching it sink.

"Be happy," Mae burst out. "You've got your whole life ahead
of you. You'll be on your own this year, no more worrying about
what your folks think."

"I'm always on my own," he'd replied.

Andy had been furious that she'd been with Danny that weekend. "The James wedding," he fumed. "And the reception at the
country club." "They'll just have to get married to a trio," Mae told
him. "I'm sure it's just as binding. I'm going to Connecticut to see
Danny." "He's your nephew, he's not your own kid." "I raised him,"
Mae replied, and what could Andy say to that?

That was an exaggeration, of course. Mae hunted up and down
her studio for the pencil she ought to have learned by now to
keep handy on her stand. She hadn't exactly raised Danny, if anyone could be said to raise children, who might do just as well if
left on their own. But she had been with him for almost a year
while Justina went through a variety of allergies and illnesses that
eventually turned out to be LeeLee. Mae had been the one in the
room when he pulled himself up to stand and finally, months later
than expected, began to walk. She learned so much about child-
hood illnesses that when LeeLee had spots on her stomach one
Thanksgiving years later, Auntie Mae was the first to guess that it
was chicken pox.

Mae plunged into the g minor scale, letting the sound of it

swoop out. The Fergusons downstairs ought to be awake by now. There was nothing wrong with living in a monastery. The conservatory had been much like one. She had spent hours and hours a day in that little practice room. A cell, really; it had just enough space for an upright piano, a chair, and a music stand. If someone opened the door without warning, it was possible to knock her over. Her friends kidded her that she concentrated so hard when she practiced that they could come in and go out again and she never noticed. But they must have made that up, Mae thought, for the door would have struck her when they opened it. Those rooms were even smaller than monks' cells.

She walked up and down in front of the ballet mirror. Her face was so solemn, chin clenched tight against the violin. Your hand must be free to move, it can't worry with holding your violin up, Professor Leon scolded. Then he would pull her left hand away from the neck of the instrument and tap the wood with two fingers, making certain she was holding it firmly. She did this with her students, and knew how it irritated them. This g minor scale; her eyes looked mournfully back at her. Justina had gotten the lively eyes, the pert expression, though age and circumstance had dulled them to sulkiness. Whenever Mae saw her, after a few months apart, she still expected to see that saucy, listening look which used to flash across Justina's face when their mother called from the kitchen. "Sister?" their mother's voice high-pitched and shrill, "Sister? I need your help in here." "Yes'm," Justina would call back respectfully, making no move from the doll teaparty and, later, the movie magazine which she was occupied with. Eventually their mother had learned to call for Mae, instead.

Mae, and Danny, too, had the long somber faces, large solemn eyes. You look so sad when you play, Professor Leon said. Is it that hard a thing to play the violin? Yes, yes, yes, she'd wanted to yell at him. And now she said the same thing to her students. Don't look so fierce. You should enjoy your music. But a monastery, all right, a boarding school, was it the best place for a seventeen-year-old to be? Daniel had been quite certain about it. Danny needed discipline, he said. Structure. He needed to calm down. But it seemed too quiet there. Mae began the opening measures of the Bach partita. It couldn't have been true that she had concentrated so hard she never heard anyone come into her practice room. Her mind wandered all over the place when her fingers worked. She didn't concentrate at all. Professor Leon had shouted at her because he said she couldn't recognize how much of her conscious intellect she had to use to play. Music is not just feeling! Not just muscles! he had shouted. Your ear and brain, they must connect. This sound is not instinctive; you must think about it, plan what you want and how to make it properly. Use your brain! Mae began the partita again; the first notes were all wrong, too lethargic. She used to stand in that practice cell while really she was on a stage soaring through the Mendelsohn Concerto, but this first phrase, it was all wrong, and she had the audience holding their breath, they loved her. It had taken so many lessons with Professor Leon yelling at her before she learned to concentrate on every note, learned to think about the way each sounded instead of letting her fingers play while her mind wandered where it would.

But surely a monastery was no place for a seventeen-year-old.

She had to get the shift in this measure so smooth that no one would hear her hand jump the two positions; Mae stood on stage behind the brilliance of the lights and no one in the dark rows of seats beyond knew that her hand had shifted, she played the phrase so perfectly, but a monastery was no place. The fifth or sixth time she tried the new fingering the thought came through so clearly that she at once laid her violin on top of the piano and went to her bedroom for stationery and a working pen. Danny needed something and she had to write him immediately.

Danny Pearson, The Carlton School, Carlton, CT.

She hunted in her desk for a stamp. She always stamped her envelope before she wrote the letter; it seemed some guarantee that she would finish it.

Dear Danny,
    I woke up this morning thinking of you.

Well, that was true enough, though it had taken till 10:45 for her to recognize it.

    I know you're glad to be back with your friends.

Especially, she thought, if the rest of his summer had been like the Memorial Day weekend she spent with them. After each meal, her brother-in-law Daniel had retreated to his third floor study, obstinately leaving the door ajar so that the entire family below had to keep their voices down and the radio off and the piano closed until late afternoon when he reappeared for iced tea and his nap on the front porch. He could, apparently, sleep through much of the noise he refused to work to. Mae had avoided the whole subject of his book after she had stupidly asked during their first supper together what he thought of the Brodie biography of Jefferson.

"Psycho-babble!" he glared at her. "It completely avoids the issues of power and political responsibility in order to play out the sexual fantasies of the so-called author." Mae made a mental note, as she returned to her plate, to remove the paperback from her shelf of bedtime reading should (as seemed unlikely) Justina and Daniel ever visit. Justina made no attempt to soften her husband's criticisms. Nor did she bother to alter the effects on the household of his demands. She was continually catching one or another of the children by the arm and lecturing them in the kitchen about their expected behavior.

"Now Danny is starting to pout like his father," she told Mae. "Half the time he acts like he doesn't hear a word I say." They sat in the living room where they were to spend the morning catching up on each other's news. Daniel had recommended it. It was pleasant enough, Mae admitted. The white starched curtains blew in and out with an early morning breeze; a shaft of sunlight made the polished wide-planked floor gleam. Justina's puckered face, bent over needlepoint, smoothed out. Justina seemed to have dismissed her irritation at Danny as soon as she brought it up, and didn't mention him again. She talked instead of household matters, of redecorating the dining room and buying fresh fruit. "I have the hardest time finding really crunchy apples," she said, and Mae found it difficult to believe that there was any other concern on her mind. Yet always, overhead, was the insistent hum of Daniel's typewriter. The humming of the machine was louder when he wasn't actually typing. Without seeming to be aware of what she did, Justina would glance up if there was too long a pause in the typing, and lose her place in what she was saying. Why, Mae won-

dered, didn't Daniel shut his door while he worked? Why didn't
Justina ask him to? After a while Mae excused herself. She really
ought to check out the music shop on Patton Ave. Andy had asked
her to find some music for him and she hadn't gotten around to
it before she left Boston. Maybe downtown. She doubted, even as
she gathered together her purse and keys and explained her rush
to Justina, she doubted that she would find what she needed. She
had taken the children there once; it was the kind of store that sold
band uniforms and bright-covered arrangements of popular songs.
But she needed time away, already, from her sister's house.

Probably, she thought, waving to Justina who stood in the doorway with her needlepoint, it was just the tension of working so
hard on his book. Her brother-in-law was quite brilliant, people
said. Justina had told her the same thing, over and over again, when
they were first married. He was under a lot of pressure all the time;
it was publish or perish, Justina said. This wasn't a good time to be
a professor of history at a branch university. Even with tenure there
were all sorts of nasty political things going on within the department which threatened Daniel's position: backstabbing. But, still.
Mae backed her car down the Pearson drive with a sense of relief,
struck that the house looked from the street like any other house
in the neighborhood. A sedate three-storied family home, its grey
paint peeling under the windows; the battered station wagon, university stickers across its bumper, parked beneath the basketball
goal; bicycles leaning against the brick wall which separated their
yard from the neighbor's. There was nothing to suggest that what
went on inside this home was any different from what went on
inside the others.

> I just wanted to remind you, (she wrote to Danny) that if you
> need a place to retreat to some weekend, there's always my apartment.
> Over your fall break, maybe, or at Thanksgiving. I'm in and out with
> rehearsals and concerts, and have students most afternoons and a few
> mornings. But you'd have a room of your own and—

She couldn't be offering up her practice room for a bedroom.
Her music room, the one place where she was completely at ease
and yet certain of her own self-discipline. One did not get drunk in
that room, for instance, though it was all right to sip sherry from a

coffee mug in there after a particularly trying student. Mae crossed out "room of your own."

You'd have a place to come back to after exploring the city.

And what adolescent in his right mind would refuse such an offer? Free room and board in a city with museums and theaters and good restaurants, an unlocked liquor cabinet (though she only kept sherry and wine and two kinds of bourbon, none of the sweet bright-colored mixtures she remembered drinking from plastic pails as a college student and supposed her nephew would prefer) and a middle-aged aunt who wouldn't say a word if he came home after midnight. Was she out of her mind? Justina would be irritated at her staking a claim on Danny's time; Daniel probably wouldn't speak to her until the last Pearson child had graduated from medical school or they all died, whichever came first.

She laid down her pen and examined her living room. Danny could sleep there easily enough. The couch would do fine, the blue couch bought with money from those Sunday-in-the-Park concerts which had nearly ruined her practice violin with the summer humidity. If she had to, she could rearrange that room around a seventeen-year-old boy.

But what would she do about Max? Who crept in and out of here on weekends and Tuesday nights like a cat slipping through its little cat door for meals. Mae tipped her chair back as far as she safely could. She had no business worrying with the life of an adolescent when she was saddled with a Max. There was a larger issue at stake here (she could hear Daniel quoting that at her) which she preferred to ignore (as Daniel would have pointed out as a fundamental character flaw). How could she claim any ability to help Danny sort out his young life when she obviously wasn't bright enough to distinguish a mature male from a baby bunting until she was stuck in a relationship? Friday afternoon and in would walk Max, his voice thinned by yet another of his perpetual minor ailments, carrying as the price of admission his one grocery bag and bottle of wine from the corner gourmet shop. (Mae bought hers in gallon jugs from the supermarket.) Wine which he wouldn't open for her until he had explained precisely what sort of bouquet she should expect from her first, slow sip. In the bag were the makings of the elaborate dinners he prepared with such meticulous enjoyment.

In the first weeks after they met, she loved being cooked for, waited on; spoiled, she called it. She was quite willing to swap her bachelor meals of canned tuna and tomatoes for Max's cooking, "multi-lingual cuisine," he called it. But as the weeks went on, his delight in chopping up plump white mushrooms, in crushing succulent cloves of garlic, in tasting with a flicker of his pointed tongue the creamy sauce from the tip of the wooden spoon he bought for her kitchen, this began to disturb her. She had expected his delighted sensuality in the kitchen to extend to other areas of her home. The first evening, savoring the smell of chicken à l'orange and fresh asparagus with real butter, she grew sufficiently relaxed over the bottles of excellent white wine to believe that his lengthy explanation of the chocolate pastry they tasted with their demitasses of espresso was intentionally pedantic. He was kidding, right? The coffee roused her just enough; the brandy he poured (into snifters brought from his own apartment; the proper glasses were essential for correct warming of the liquor) seemed the perfect prelude to the next entertainment. Mae curled up on the couch beside him, her knees bare and bent, her shoes off. She twirled the almost-empty brandy snifter dreamily in one hand, and with the other just touched the curl of light hair at the back of his neck. Surely, now; she wrapped her finger into the curl and tugged it gently, pressing her palm against his neck.

Max held on to his brandy with both hands, resting it squarely on his stomach between sips. He gave a sigh which was half-belch, half final gasp of relaxation after heavy labor, and closed his eyes. "What a meal," he said, sotto voce. "Excellent."

She'd waited. She was certain he found her attractive. He kept coming back, he eyed her hungrily over the grocery sack. On each date, before his arrival, she decided all over again that Max was simply insecure about revealing emotion. There were plenty of men who became embarrassed when they tried to talk of love. Perhaps, despite his confidence in the kitchen and the blasé, man-of-the-world way in which he referred to his job "in business," he just didn't know what to do about women. And, after all, it had been that hint of lost-little-boy in his wide-browed beautiful face which had first attracted her to him. It was up to her to take the initiative. She had trained herself, after too many relationships where her needs were clearly second fiddle, to be a little bolder. But she had never managed, in the months and months they had been dining together, to seize the moment and grab the groceries from him before they absorbed his attention and his energy.

It was past time she was dressed and out the door. Good old Andy, he always waited, but she hated to test him too far. Mae stepped into her tallest sandals and pulled a brilliant red cotton sundress over her head, fastening the flat white buttons up the front and clipping in earrings as she limped, sandals not yet buckled, to the door. She checked her reflection in the slanting window of the pharmacy beside her apartment, making sure she'd done up all those buttons. Not that Andy would care what she looked like. His preference was more for the other sex, a fact which had destroyed his marriage. But still. Mae hobbled as fast as her heels would allow towards the bus stop.

"There you are, sweetheart. Only fifteen minutes late this time." Andy leaned on one elbow against the mahogany lectern which shielded the maitre d' from his guests. A reading lamp, neck curved low, threw a circle of light onto the reservation book, repeated in two blinding circles in the host's eyeglasses. He straightened up, seeing Mae, gave a quick nod to Andy, and glided into the shadows of the restaurant, bearing with him a stack of red-bound menus as if for protection.

Andy pushed the rolled sleeves of his cream shirt further up his arms and bent to brush Mae's cheek with a kiss.

"Oh, Andy, I'm sorry I've made you wait again. I was in the middle of a letter and forgot all about the time."

"Not to worry. I've had time to forget the traffic on the way over." His grey eyes, beneath light hair trained to rise smoothly from the broad forehead, rested on her with the benevolence of an old uncle. "Shall we?" he asked, placing his hand beneath her elbow as if requesting permission for a dance. He guided her through the narrow doorway into the darker restaurant, moved them deftly past crowded tables and waiters with trays poised a bit too ostentatiously over their heads, bringing her, with a final half-turn, safely to a white-clothed table in the farthest corner. He drew out a wicker chair.

"But there's already someone—" Mae began.

Half-hidden by the tall carafe of wine, a man looked up at her. His was an angular face, the skin stretching taut across the cheekbones, temples thin, hollowed out. Yet the expression of this face was more stern than sorrowful, as if it had known not just the sufferings of himself a prisoner but had seen too many others in that state. From the deep recesses beneath the jutting forehead, dark eyes glinted at her. Mae felt her own quail before them. They were the no-color of all color concentrated together; closest, she thought, to the blue-black sheen of coal sparkling in the sun. Mae dropped gratefully into the chair Andy nudged, ever-so-gently, against the backs of her knees.

"Mae, this is Jason Dewar." Andy pulled his own chair between the two of them and sprawled back into it, keeping his palms face down on the arms, elbows bent, as if ready to spring up if need be.

Jason Dewar! The name leapt out at her from the backs of dozens of albums. Black, businesslike letters against white backgrounds; Cleveland Symphony Orchestra, Jason Dewar conducting. More recently, with a smaller orchestra somewhere in the northeast, she couldn't remember which. International tours in which he was featured with top-ranking orchestras. And a new recording label; his name in white letters, still small; unobtrusive print that took his fame for granted. No need to trumpet his presence. Jason Dewar, conductor. Why hadn't Andy warned her?

"You'll forgive me for intruding on what I understand to be a weekly lunch date." His voice was low, rough, with an assurance which turned his apology into a declaration of intent. "I was at your concert last night and wanted to find out more about your quartet. I introduced myself to Andy afterwards. We found a great deal to say to one another, and he suggested that I come to lunch today and meet you."

He accepted Mae's hand across the table with a nod that was almost a bow.

"We've all been looking forward to your arrival at the university, Mr. Dewar. My students tell me that the university orchestras have been desperate for a strong conductor. They're eager for their first rehearsal with you."

He bent his head, in perfunctory acknowledgement of her welcome, ignoring her summary of student gossip as he did her rather-formal smile. Mae guessed that he had already endured as many comments about what the orchestra needed as he had fluttering greetings from the faculty wives.

He didn't bother with chit-chat. "I'm hoping you'll join the faculty ensemble, Miss Cavin, as a salaried musician. We need a strong first violinist since Dr. Finney's wife left with him. After hearing you play last night, I'm quite sure you will do."

"Are you now." If he noticed her tone, he didn't show it.

"Quite sure. Andy thought you'd be interested in the idea. That's why I bring it up. He seems to feel your career is ready for a new turn."

"Does he now."

Andy pressed his palms a little more firmly into the arms of his chair.

Mae's voice was sweet. "But I'm afraid I never play in groups of more than five or six, Mr. Dewar, if I can help it at all. Thank you for the offer, anyway."

"Come on, Mae." Andy pushed himself forward, springing from the back of the chair to lean, hands clasped between his knees, close to her. "You need more students. The quartet needs more bookings. The faculty ensemble will give you more exposure and some publicity for us. And it wouldn't hurt you to learn some orchestral repertoire."

She turned on him. "Is there something about my playing you would like to discuss with me?"

"Mae." It was a very gentle rebuke. "The money wouldn't hurt you, either."

"Mr. Dewar can't be interested in my personal finances." She sat straight against the wicker back and smiled at the two men like a debutante choosing her dinner escort. "I have plenty of students, and I am quite able to take care of myself. Thank you."

"In that case, you might consider playing for free." Mr. Dewar's voice, as carefully polite as hers, hid a thread of laughter.

Mae wanted to make him understand. "It's just that I've never been able to stand the sort of time-wasting that goes on in large

rehearsals. People drifting in late, learning their parts as they go
along, the whole group at a standstill while the conductor teaches
them in public what they should have learned on their own."

"I assure you, Miss Cavin, I have little enough time myself to
want to waste any of it in superfluous rehearsal." There was little
doubt about the coldness in his tone.

She hadn't meant to insult him. "In an orchestra, you're told
what to play and when. And how, if the conductor thinks he knows
something about your instrument. Which sometimes he does," she
added hastily. "I can't hear myself in a large group. I have no control
over the sound. I'm just one more filler-in. But in our quartet, or
on my own, there's no one who will play exactly as I can, good
or bad." She fumbled for the right words. "I'm just not a team
musician."

"Meaning I'm the team coach." He shrugged and looked at
Andy. Mae realized that he had no idea what it was like to be buried
in a crowd of sound, to be a mere blurred part of a massive whole,
an insignificance which made her dizzy. By profession it was he
who ruled the crowd; he stood alone above them all. His very
whisper was like a shouted command, a jerk of his mouth or flick
of his finger would be scrutinized and clung to for direction by
them all.

Andy laid his hand on hers. "Mr. Dewar suggested that you
might want to take on a few of the graduate students for your own."

Mae turned to the conductor. "But I'm not on the faculty."

"We could work around that, I think. If you want to teach and
you are a good teacher, there are always students who need you.
You'd have to use your own studio, of course. I haven't been here
long enough, yet," and in the bemused way he added that last word
it was clear that he was so accustomed to getting his own way
that mere length of time wouldn't deter him long, "to feel free to
arrange it otherwise."

"I understand." Mae smiled with relief at the waiter who stood
silently behind Andy. "Let me think about it, all right?"

He didn't speak to her again throughout the meal.

Mae didn't even spend an hour with them. She fled; there was
no other word for it. She had to practice. Yes, she would call Andy
first thing in the morning. Certainly, she would let Mr. Dewar know

as soon as possible what she decided to do.

The wall of midafternoon heat, held as in a vise between the cement sidewalk and the low grey ceiling of sky, struck her as she stepped from the coffeeshop. What startled her was not so much the heat, you got used to that by misdsummer and though from there it only got worse, you believed that it would be over soon, in a month, six weeks. It might be cooler next week. The shock was the noise, a barrage of sound with no distinct origin and no discernible end. Though cars roared past and vanished down the street, the roaring continued. Tires bumped over a manhole in front of her, the metal cover rattling against the metal rim; trucks hissed and clashed into gear. For moments at a time, no cars drove past on this side of the street, but the noise never stopped. It was as though a great choir, commanded to hold a chord, kept staggering their breathing so that the audience never saw all mouths at once take in a breath and it seemed as though they sustained the sound forever without pause. It could kill you, this noise, Mae thought as she stepped into it. Or at least drive you a little crazy. Indeed, the people around her hurrying back to offices were bowed down, moving only by necessity in that desperate hour after lunch when time and the sun together stand still overhead. While in the darkened coffeeshop, people lingered, and you knew the chime of a silver spoon against a glass of tea, and the soft thud as your own waiter lifted plates back to his tray and set out cups for coffee.

Mae pushed past businessmen, grateful to have something tangible to fight against. That man, the great Jason Dewar, staring her down like he was some fierce Old Testament prophet passing judgment. Andy had let him; Andy hadn't even called her to let her know ahead of time that he'd invited that man along. The two of them had interrupted the rhythm of her week. She was supposed to have her Friday morning and then the quiet lunch with Andy in preparation for the weekend. She had no intention of letting herself be lost in an orchestra. But the suggestion that she ought to, Andy's hints that it would be good for her, the great man's invitation, these surged through her mind and spoiled her solitude. Now that she knew she might do, ought to do, something else, she was not so sure about the perfection of her independence. A few more students, good ones, and she could start saving for a decent car. Good, older students, certain in their profession; she could teach difficult music and arrange real recitals which other musicians would attend, none of the tactful negotiations with mothers hungry for proof of a child prodigy.

But Andy should have called her. Mae turned down the quieter block where her apartment building stood. They talked almost every day. Sometimes they called first thing in the morning, when each knew the other would be home alone, each lying in his or her respective double bed, phone tucked between pillows and ear, hands (hers) twisting the phone cord in lieu of the cigarettes he forbade her to smoke. When they were too sleepy to talk, they sometimes stayed on the line anyway, comforted just lying there in a silence shared by another person. After her first dinner with Max, they'd discussed him until almost dawn; when they were fighting with their previous violist before they found Nonnie Gardener and her husband, they'd spent hours on the phone after quartet rehearsal calming each other down. Andy called her after he visited his children, though he never talked about his ex-wife. Mae didn't even know her name. Nor did he tell her anything about his male friends, as though still reluctant to trust some things to a woman. But he might have mentioned that he was bringing Jason Dewar to lunch.

The phone rang as she slammed the door of her apartment.

"Psychic," she muttered, peeling off her sandals and leaving them in the middle of the hall, as she rushed to the studio. "Hello. It's a bit late to tell me about him now, isn't it?"

"I'm sorry, sweetheart. I honestly didn't think you'd mind if I brought him. I thought you might even enjoy having another man along."

"Right." Mae searched through the drawer of the telephone table for a cigarette. "It didn't occur to you that I might want to know about it beforehand."

"I didn't think he'd spring the idea of the ensemble on you so quickly."

"Was that your idea or his?" Not even a match; she banged the drawer shut.

"I know you need the money. I know you'd like some challenging students. And I don't think your reputation would suffer from introductions to the university crowd."

"Who are afraid to sight-read a new piece of music unless they have clearance from the dean, the chancellor, and the state arts council. And, as of last week, from the great Jason Dewar. Excuse me, he must be Dr. Dewar now that he's with the university."

"Your cynicism is showing."

"Cynicism." Mae hooted. "You're the one who wants me to turn into a groupie so the quartet can get some publicity."

"We could use some bookings that pay. Think of the university kids, all those class reunions and fraternities dripping money. When they give a party they could pay whatever we wanted just for the prestige of having their own live string quartet set up behind the bar."

"So you play with the ensemble."

"Jason Dewar doesn't need another cellist. He needs you. Mae, what do you have in the bank right now?"

"None of your business."

"It is my business. I don't want to lose our first violinist to the credit bureau. Or lose the free meals I get at your house."

"They're not free. I pay through the nose for them by being nice to Max." At the thought of Max's face, anxious over a pot on the stove, pushing away steam which rose to his face, she had to smile. She imagined that Jason Dewar must concentrate like that also, fanning away like flies all minor annoyances—disputes over chairs, missing music, whether or not she ought to have the privilege of teaching the graduate students when she had no ties with the department.

"I know you don't like anyone telling you what to do, Mae, but for my sake I wish you'd be practical."

"I am practical." She lowered her voice; he was only trying to look out for her. "I didn't buy that black dress in Saks' window this afternoon, I'm so practical. I'm still eating curried shrimp and wild rice from Max's last extravaganza, I'm so practical. I'm always practical."

"Then take this job offer more seriously." He hung up before she could answer.

When she went into her bedroom to throw her sandals into the closet, there was the letter she'd begun that morning, its pages curling in the afternoon humidity. "You'd have a place to come back to." She couldn't remember writing that, though the words were in her large backhand strokes. The sentences looked alien; she couldn't recall what had prompted her to write them. With a quick grunt of impatience, she tore the page in two.

What business was it of hers what Danny did? He was almost a man, he was perfectly capable of running his own life his own way. Men always did. Whatever uneasiness she had woken under that morning now seemed silly, over-imaginative after this afternoon's realities—the heat and Jason Dewar's request. It embarrassed her to think of how worked-up she'd gotten over nothing. Had she been that emotional with Jason Dewar? Surely Andy would have told her just now if she'd seemed absurd. Mae picked the pieces of the letter off the floor. Daniel always said that Danny could take care of himself. He had scolded Justina last spring for trying to call him during an epidemic of flu which put him in the school infirmary.

"He's old enough to look after himself. Leave him alone. Or he might as well still be at home with his mommy running around after him." Daniel's hand was flat against the telephone. Justina didn't push him away, and Daniel said nothing more, perhaps because she, Mae, was in the study with them.

Probably Daniel was right. Probably what she had intended to do would be babying Danny, standing between him and his growing up. Whatever he was passing through now was his own, and she shouldn't intrude with her own interpretation of what he needed, her own memories of teenage anxieties. He would have to create his own solutions, or his maturity would be only an imitation of someone else's. And anyway, she didn't really know what it was young men had to go through in order to grow up. She shouldn't be giving advice to a nephew she saw a few times a year, no matter how close she'd been to him when he was a baby. She was exaggerating her importance in his life, the same way she exaggerated everything else. The way she'd exaggerated Max's mild interest in her into something deeper; the way she'd imagined, before Max, that Owen Lewis was in love with her. She was sick of the way her imagination confused her, ruining her relationships since the reality was always so disappointing in comparison to what she had thought was real. She ought to grow out of that.

Mae tore the remains of the letter to confetti and let the bits flutter to the trash can.

At 7:30, Max appeared, before she remembered to call him and say she was too tired to eat. She left him in the kitchen, puttering with his food processor, and went to select some jazz albums. She stacked them ruthlessly on the stereo, then interrupted Max to ask for some wine. "Make sure you let it breathe first!" he warned. "Red wine has to breathe to reach its true quality." A marvelous bouquet; she sipped, no, drank it down. A fine wine. She let the music pour over her with the warmth of that first glass. After a while she leaned against the frame of the kitchen door and watched Max work. He was stirring something on the stove, actually humming a little to himself, humming against the rhythm of the jazz which had taken possession of her, imposing its pulse upon her own. It was the sound of Max humming a popular song against the beat of good jazz that ended it. Mae felt the power of her body against the door frame, the curve of her waist and hip flattened against the wood. "Be quiet," she said.

"Hmmm?" He didn't look up. Mae leaned over to the kitchen table and grabbed the wine bottle, sloshing wine into her glass, drinking it as steadily down. Then she walked carefully over to the stove and waited beside him, her hip in the silky grey dress just touching his.

"How's the wine?" he asked, his voice distant and abstracted, that of a man with important business to perform.

"Fine, the wine's fine." Very gently she set her glass down on the counter; then, just as deliberately, reached across him and turned the burner off, jerking the saucepan away from the heat.

"It's almost done," he said, alarmed, pushing her away.

"There are other rooms in this apartment besides the kitchen, Max." She thrust herself between him and the stove, not an easy task, for he was tall and strongly built and worried about his cream sauce. Mae wrapped her arms around him to pull him close, and felt him peer over her shoulder at the saucepan. She began to laugh, at Max, at her attempts to interest him, at herself for hanging on to him and then she turned back to retrieve her glass of wine, and finished it and went and found her coat and put it on and told him, "I'm going out. I'm going out to the movies. When I come home, I want dinner cleaned up and you and your gourmet entourage out of here for good. Vamoose."

She had to watch as comprehension spread across his wide pale face like slow cake mix in a pan. She couldn't remember how she ever met him in the first place. "Goodbye, Max," she said quietly.

She stood in Andy's doorway and told him about it. "Why am I always so dumb about men? I kept thinking that Max just needed a little encouragement. When really he wasn't interested in anything except my appreciation of his cooking."

"We did get some fine meals out of him." Andy led her inside and closed the door.

"I keep doing this to myself. I'm no better now than I was in college. I told you about my theory teacher. God, I was in love with him. I lived for class: forty minutes, Monday, Wednesday, Friday. I washed my hair every day and wore black because I wanted to look like a graduate student. And the only way I could get him to notice me was to be late for class. I was late to every single one. But he always stopped his lecture when I came in. I nearly flunked theory that semester. I couldn't concentrate on what he said, I was too busy concentrating on him. And I couldn't go to office hours and get help. I couldn't see him alone. Though I used to walk up and down the hall thinking that maybe today I'd have the nerve to go in."

"There's an old Bogey and Bacall movie on." Andy said. "Let's see what real romance looks like."

"Maybe," Mae said during the first commercial," maybe I need someone of my own so much that I project the man I want on every man I meet." Andy nodded, turning the sound back up as the movie came back on. In the next commercial he put his arm around her. "Someday," he said, the images on the screen flickering aimlessly past, "you'll find the right man who'll take care of you in all the right ways, even better than you imagined."

"You sound like my sister Justina. Eternally hopeful that life will change."

"Well, hey," he said. "She's got the right idea."

Mae slit the plastic wrapping with her thumbnail and very gently took out the record, balancing it between her fingertips as she placed it on the turntable. She turned the volume way up (Mrs. Ferguson had taken the baby out shopping. Mae had heard her clattering down the stairs with the stroller) and quickly sat down as the needle bumped into place. There was a rustle of static, and then the music, as loving an opening as there could be, the strings so clear, so perfectly together, that the chords fell as one note, as if a single hand plucked out, in one swift grasp, the harmonies. The phrase rose and soared with such boundless joy that Mae could have flown with the sound. But she sat perfectly still in her blue armchair and pictured, instead, the arms that created this sound. Not the musicians, their black sleeves flapping; not them. But the beckoning arms of the man who led them, his arms closed here for the pianissimo, holding the orchestra down, quiet, but never still; then opening out like a rising sun, allowing the sound to grow until there was nothing he could do to hold it back and the sound rose triumphant and his arms simply followed, bursting apart in great circles in the air, opening in joyous circles that embraced the air, embraced the sound, embraced the circle of musicians below him.

It would seem so easy, watching him. The audience behind would see his arms flowing through the air in continual patterns which would be the music before they even heard a sound. The music would appear to follow so effortlessly that even Dr. Finney's orchestra might, under such a conductor, dream of sounding like that.

The stereo clicked off. Mae picked up the album cover she had pored so long over in the record store. She had put it back and left twice, walked hurriedly down the street. She was supposed to buy stockings, some rosin, a wide hair-clip. She already had a good recording of Beethoven's Seventh. But this was Jason Dewar's recording. She left the stockings on the lingerie counter and rushed back to the record store. The clerk probably thought she was crazy. As she paid for the album, the cashier informed her that Jason Dewar had moved to town. "He's rented an apartment in this neighborhood. Had you heard he'll be working with the university orchestra?" "Really?" Mae echoed. "What a pity. I understand that everyone just adored Dr. Finney." She swept out for the last time, her purchase held tightly in both hands.

There was a tiny picture of him on the back cover. The photographer had caught him with his face tipped to the left, encouraging a player he must have liked, for his eyes were gentle and held at once expectation and forgiveness that the note had not emerged as purely as it might. His hands, palms up, reached towards his orchestra as delicately, as purposefully, as a ballerina's.

What would it be like to be a part of that sound? Mae put the recording on again.

The quartet played Sunday night at the Spider and the Fly, a vegetarian restaurant with a front entrance several steps below the sidewalk. Because of the heat, no one sat on the patio, but crowded inside on narrow wooden benches like church pews which faced each other across thick oaken tables on which regular customers carved initials, dates, and the wistful opening lines of never-finished poetry. It was a place which Mae poked fun at, a cream-cheese-dill-on-healthy-pumpernickel sort of place which didn't pay them much, but they enjoyed playing there because the manager saved them plenty of room to spread out, no matter how crowded the restaurant was. That was refreshing; Andy claimed that in some places waiters dropped salad dressing on his cello as they squeezed past.

The university was in summer session, and Mae busied herself typecasting faces by departments as she waited for the Gardeners to finish tuning. A gang of incoming freshmen in crisp bright sports shirts moved restlessly in the doorway looking for a table. They finally settled down near the bar, poking at one another, their thick muscular necks red as though they were aware that they were being scrutinized by customers not quite accustomed to their type in here. Mae admired them for staying, and kept an eye on them at intervals during the music. They all talked at once, very fast and loud, telling each other some long joke about the tallest boy whom they embraced as they rocked with laughter. She didn't think they'd noticed that there was a quartet playing. When the waitress set down their second large pitcher of beer they tried to pull her into the joke, too, not quite flirting with her, their eyes above their opened mouths eager for her approval. Something about them reminded her of the boys she'd watched in the dining hall line at Danny's school—the same startled pleasure at finding themselves the center of attention, their growing hilarity at their own wit, their absolute belief that the noise they made was so good-natured, so appealing, that everyone around must appreciate it, too.

Mae was sorry that the manager went over to the boys during the first break and requested that they leave before the music began again.

She pulled his sleeve as he passed. "They weren't that loud, Bill. We could play over them."

He paused beside her and swung a vague glance around at his customers. "Somebody complained; he wanted to hear the music. They can always come back when they grow up."

It was in the middle of their third Haydn (nothing too dense in this weather, at this hour: Brahms was out of the question, Beethoven chancey) that she noticed Jason Dewar in a corner booth. At the page turn, she flicked another glance at him. He was sliding a glass from side to side between those famous hands, apparently absorbed in seeing whether it would slide on its own once he had given it a starting push. Mae dropped her eyes to her music; she had nearly missed an entrance. As soon as the piece was through, she tapped Andy's knee with her bow.

"Did you invite him here, too?" she whispered. "The great Jason

Dewar." She nodded behind his head.

"People who like good music know instinctively where we are," Andy whispered back. To her embarrassment, he turned in his chair, gripping the neck of his cello with his left hand, and waved his bow at the conductor. Jason Dewar waved back, a brief salute that acknowledged their presence but managed to convey that he was perfectly content to sit in a bar at night alone. Certainly he would not expect them to join him at their next break. But ought they absolutely to ignore him?

He resolved Mae's fretting by appearing beside them when they stood to stretch after "The Hunt" quartet.

"It sounds pretty good." His hand rested on the back of Mae's chair. "Not as polished as last Thursday."

"This is hardly a concert hall." Andy grinned. He introduced the Gardeners. "Our second violin and viola."

"A fine viola sound." Jason Dewar nodded at Nonnie Gardener. "You have a rich, lush tone. You must have started as a viola player, not one of the many who begin on the violin and switch over. You can always hear the difference in tone." To her husband, he said nothing. Mae bent over her violin, rubbing it hard with a cloth. To cover the silence until the Gardeners moved away, Andy returned to Jason Dewar's first comment.

"We don't worry overmuch about perfection when we play in restaurants. We're not paid enough, for one thing, and so we use places like this to enjoy our music, sometimes to try things out we aren't ready to perform. If they like what they hear, what they can hear," Andy's hand indicated the rattle of conversations and dishes," maybe they'll pay to come to a real performance. We'd prefer that, to have an audience concentrating only on the music. And so does the manager; if we play too brilliantly, no one will feel comfortable eating."

Jason Dewar shrugged, pulled out a thin pack of imported cigarettes which he tilted in turn to Andy and to Mae (she looked at Andy and refused) before shaking one out for himself. "A pity," he remarked, lighting it. He breathed in, then continued through a cloud of smoke. "They ought to make up their minds which they want. Conversation or good music. A compromise won't allow much of either one." His smile flashed out. "But you have an interesting marketing strategy. Let me know how it works." And he was gone, stepping lightly through the crowded restaurant.

"Did I shock him away?" Andy asked. "No," he answered himself. He took Mae's violin from her and set it in its case. "You don't shock someone who is one of the best conductors in the country and knows it. Let's go find our free drinks."

Neither spoke much on the walk back to her apartment. They could hear the buzz of each street lamp as they moved from one pool of light to the next. Usually that sound would have lulled Mae into complete relaxation by the time they reached her building. Tonight it was an irritant. Andy was keyed up, too. He strode along quickly, almost a full step in front of her, and seemed annoyed when he remembered to slow down. The silence between them was tense with unspoken thoughts.

"Come up, Andy."

He shook his head. "I've got the kids tomorrow, and I'd better get some sleep."

"You have them all day, then."

"Until six. I'm not allowed to feed them supper." His voice was bitter.

"Well, that's still plenty of time for them to wreck your apartment and get you out shopping for new toys."

"I guess. I miss them, Mae."

All she could do was give him a one-armed hug and watch as he walked back down to the corner. It had been sheer luck that she met him. A woman she knew from the Music Teachers Association had insisted that she attend her spring recital. Andy's daughter was the first on the program, a chubby, curly-headed blond bearing no resemblance to his lean sardonic self. The little girl glowed in her delight at sitting before a roomful of grownups who were as dressed up as she and all watching her. She kicked her polished patent leather toes in gleeful rhythm against the piano as accompaniment to the brief piece she played. Mrs. Minn had to fetch her away from the piano after the applause had stopped.

"Yes, that one's mine." Andy returned Mae's smile across the refreshment table, then looked with silent dismay at the lime-sherbet-thickened punch which gleamed in the crystal bowl. "Do you suppose there's anything else a proud parent might drink?"

She knew he was a musician before he told her. There was something about the way he listened to her, tilting his head a bit to one side as if reckoning the timbre of her voice, deciding what key she might sound best in, what range she might encompass. He asked her first. "Violin or viola?"

"How did you know? Oh, of course." She touched the inevitable red mark beneath her chin where the instrument chafed. "A hazard of the profession."

"That, and a sub-standard income," he agreed.

"How do you know about that?" she had countered, for he was as well-dressed as any in that roomful of businessmen and university professors and their wives.

Then had begun a discussion of their work, their money worries, their backgrounds, which continued while Jennifer reappeared to lean against her father's legs and stare impatiently at this strange lady who was interrupting her first recital celebration, then continued over supper the next week. Later, Andy called to ask her to fill in for the missing violinist in his quartet, a position she inherited for good when the woman moved to New York. Since that meeting, she hadn't had time to despair over whether or not she would ever make a living from her music. The quartet played continually, if not always profitably, and Andy was a good business manager and an unending source of suggestions about where to pick up better students.

But what was it about musicians which always alerted you to what they were? Andy and Mae discussed that, too. There had to be a disdain for money, a self-protective scorn for those who worked only to be well-fed and better dressed. A cavalier attitude towards the way things—themselves—looked, acquired perhaps from so many hours alone listening to oneself play the same passage over and over again. Hopefully, a sense of humor: self-ridicule and cynicism in some, disappointment soured to bitterness in others, which came of work so minute in a world which, for respectability's sake, demanded grandeur. Above all, concentration: the ability to focus completely on one tiny thing, with a kind of pinpoint hearing like a jeweller's vision when wearing his glass. While their reward was, what? A sonata played as perfectly as possible.

More likely, a phrase or maybe two played well, followed by many more passages of mediocre sound as uninspired, as deadening, as the fill-in-the-blank string scales in a brass-happy Sousa march. If you were sane enough to have no self-delusions you knew you'd keep falling short of what you wanted to achieve. There was no way you could take too many things seriously, then, so accustomed were you to accepting defeat in the only realm that to your heart and ears and mind had any importance.

If it hadn't been for Andy, she would long ago have quit trying to support herself in that world and become, instead, a secretary at one of the universities, playing music on occasional weekends and able to afford tickets to all the best concerts. Andy was everything she had needed in a colleague and a friend. And yet—Mae let herself into her apartment, her mind racing with a new discontent. It was an excuse for pacing; she moved aimlessly through the rooms, turning up the air conditioner when she passed it, brushing out her hair to rid it of the smell of cigarettes, switching on all the lights and checking behind the doors, though if anyone had come in while she was out, if there was anyone here now, knowing about it wouldn't help her any. Mae undressed as she walked, leaving her earrings on the mantel in the living room, her shoes in the kitchen, her watch on the cabinet where she paused at last for a glass and the bottle of sherry. Jason Dewar had left the restaurant in order to meet a woman, she decided as she sipped. Someone elegant, of course, tall and very thin, and so wealthy that she had lots of time to concentrate on her appearance. Her skin would exude perfume from every pore. Perfume which had been creamed and massaged in, not merely sprayed around in the last hurried dash out the door. Those who sat in the dark auditorium near her listening to Jason Dewar's music would know by the soft waves of perfume and the whisper of sheer hosiery as she crossed and re-crossed her legs that a beautiful woman was nearby.

Mae sighed. She shouldn't have been so rude to Max. He was a more-than-presentable dinner companion. He was soothing to be around, as long as she didn't expect too much from him. She had rushed him past what he was comfortable with. Maybe a few more evenings and he would have loosened up. Maybe she ought to call him and apologize. Midnight; a little after. It wasn't that late. She stood before the phone, chewing her thumb, then traced down the list of numbers on the wall. Skipping over Max's name, she dialed Connecticut before she quite understood what she had done.

As she listened to the phone ring, far away, she thought of how silly she would sound. She had no reason for calling except the vague feeling she'd awakened with one morning last week. It would probably mortify him when she tried to explain. Hi, Danny, this is your Auntie Mae. I'm calling because I had a dream about you the other day. Though it hadn't been a dream. It was more concrete than that, less mystical. It had been intuition.

She doubted if he would understand her sense of responsibility for him. He had been too young to remember their year together. He would not have known what an anchor his small, firm body had been for her then. She had been floating around, just out of graduate school, bored with the little orchestras that offered her jobs and unable to compete for positions in the larger ones; she hadn't been ready then to accept the fact that she was a good but not a great musician and that her living would likely depend upon training other women's children to be the musicians she had dreamed of becoming. Then suddenly there was Danny needing to be changed, or Danny holding up his hands and demanding "walk," or Danny peeking up at her from her bed where he was supposedly napping, or Danny reaching out to her with a smudged fistful of chocolate cake, his highest offering, and she had forgotten about all the other. She had no such bond to LeeLee or to Nathan. She bought them ice cream cones and took them for long drives when she visited, but they were not a part of her.

"Carlton School? Yes? Is this Granville Hall? I'm looking for Danny Pearson. He's on the fourth floor, I think. Room 401. Would you mind running up to see if he's awake?"

"No problem," a boy's light voice assured her, "N.P." She heard the thud as he dropped the phone against the wall, and the distant sound of a scuffle.

"Is that the pizza man?"

"Nah. Some female for Dann-o."

"Well, come on. If we don't get our order in they won't deliver. No deliveries after one."

"Can't help it. Dann-o's got a woman on the line."

Four flights up, Mae thought, and I bet they don't bother to walk up and find him. Just you try to hang up on me, buster.

"Dann-o." The yell became fainter. He's actually going up. Bless you, honey; the walk will do you good.

"Dann-o Pearson. Some woman wants you. On the phone."

After a while the chortles grew louder again. The phone was picked up and the same light voice apologized. "Sorry. He must really be sacked out. Do you want to leave a message?"

"Thanks, no." She thought fleetingly of the wasted long distance charges. But any message would get garbled in the argument over pepperoni versus sausage. As she hung up, a deep voice was groaning, "Aw, man, hurry up. We shoulda got our order in two minutes ago."

Danny had called home in the middle of her visit there last fall. She had been teaching LeeLee and Nathan how to play Rook when Justina hissed, "Danny's on the phone!" over the receiver, slicing their game into silence. Across the room, Daniel turned his book face down and laid it on the arm of his chair and went to stand near the doorway where Justina talked to their son. He kept his back to them, hands in the pockets of the silk robe he wore for evening reading, turning his head every once in a while as if studying the shapes of the trees outside. But Mae sensed that he was alert to every word his wife spoke to their son, that he was straining also to catch the voice at the other end.

"Let me talk to him!" LeeLee pulled at her mother and was finally allowed the phone. "Did you get my letter? Did you ask any of your friends if they want somebody to write to them? I read about these girls that wrote to soldiers in Europe during the war." There followed some long, patient, elder-brother explanation to which LeeLee clung, breathing loudly through her mouth. The pink splotches on her face grew brighter. Beside her, Nathan waited quietly for his turn. When she handed him the phone, his joy rang out in the one word he spoke, as if he had been the one homesick. "Danny?" He said nothing more, but kept nodding, as if by that action to keep his brother talking to him. Mae was struck by the way he seemed to cradle the receiver, almost shielding it with his body, like some wild beast her young. She understood this better a moment later, when Justina beckoned her to the phone.

"Say a word to your nephew," she whispered.

They talked of nothing in particular: Danny told her some long story of sleeping through too many eight o'clock classes and almost getting put on probation; she recounted a similar incident from her days at the conservatory. Neither of them suggested the possibility that school was not an entirely pleasant experience, nor mentioned the factor of homesickness. Neither said anything which possibly could have been interpreted as questioning Daniel's decision to send Danny away. But it bothered her, the feeling that every word she said and some of Danny's were shared among the two adults who hovered behind her, seeming almost not to breathe until the last crackle of static had faded. Then they wanted to discuss Danny with her, and prodded her for every word he had told her about school. LeeLee barricaded herself behind several books, holding one before her face and stacking several others on her lap; Nathan had disappeared as soon as he got off the phone. When she decently could, Mae went up to her room.

Mae's hand still rested on the telephone. Calling a man put you in such a ridiculous position. He would think she was chasing him. At her age she ought to have more self-respect. But he was the great Jason Dewar; he knew that he was far beyond her reach. And he had liked her playing. Rather breathlessly this time, Mae dialed the number he had given her. He picked up the phone after one ring.

"Mr. Dewar?"

"Yes?" His voice was curt, but quite awake. He must have been working right beside the phone.

"Mr. Dewar, this is Mae Cavin. I promised to let you know as soon as I decided about the orchestra. Well, I'd like to join, at least for the fall."

"That's fine. The next rehearsal is Monday at 7:30. We begin on time."

"I'll be there," she promised. Her voice, it almost sang.

Danny lay in bed, rigid. Let them pound on the door. They could pound on it all night if they wanted to. "There's a female for you, Dann-o," one of them yelled. Right. He was sick of their endless joking around. He couldn't walk into the bathroom in the morning without having to listen to a bunch of wisecracks. They were so full of themselves, these guys. They couldn't even use each other's real names, but had to abbreviate, elaborate, until the stodgiest student, renamed, came off sounding like an executive shooting the breeze over the phone. Hiya, pal, what's doin'. William H. Stanley (the fourth) was Wills; Tim Dewar was, hit the syllable hard and shoot it from your mouth like a football cheer, Doo. Danny they called Dann-o. Rob Barclay, the senior proctor, had given him the name last year at the dorm party held to welcome new boys. Rob Barclay, called Bob Barker because of his never-failing talk-show-host good spirits, had raced up and down the dormitory stairs this morning like a hyperactive squirrel, flinging his toothy grin and emphatic "how ARE you?" over his shoulder as he passed Danny still plodding up the four flights to his room. Rob/Bob had paused on the second floor landing to adjust his tie in the mirror which hung there, giving Danny one moment to contemplate his reply. "Fuck off," came quickest to mind; "I'm just shitty, thanks," next. But Rob/Bob had leapt down the stairs before Danny could speak, waving, cheerily, as he went.

For awhile Danny had been intrigued by the possibility of creating a personality to go with his new name. Dann-o Pearson was

someone confident and cocksure, down to the swing of the knapsack over his right shoulder after class. Dann-o was tough but graceful; his hand waited for the last split second to pluck the football
from the air. Every move fitted the man. But over the last year, even
more in this, the nickname became just one more thing which
was alien to him, which demanded of him that he be other than
he was. Whatever that might be. He was an alien—at the word he
watched antennae spring from his forehead, high-pitched beeps
pour from his mouth—he didn't fit at home, he didn't fit here. He
didn't know any place where he belonged.

The guys were so weird up here. They weren't bothered by
having to wear jackets and ties to class and to meals, even on Satur-
days. They pulled on soft yellow or pale striped sweaters that at
home would get you called a fag. They rushed into classes like they
really wanted to be there, talking in staccato bursts about music
they'd heard in "the city," about movies he'd never heard of which
they called "films." They caught "the shuttle" back and forth to the
city on weekends. Danny lived in a city, too, he'd thought, until
one weekend last spring when James Fordham (Ham) took him
home for a weekend to the city. From then on, educated, Danny
could see that Asheville was nothing but a hicktown, ringed by a
hodgepodge of shopping malls and Pizza Huts, and for fun you
drove from one to the other. Without a car you stayed home. In
New York, people walked to see films; there were even buses. The
nose-catching stink of the Canton paper mill, which had always
intrigued him, became an irritant: Asheville couldn't even get its
pollution right; its smells, like his accent, were a little too obvious,
a little too simple. Asheville had too many churches, and people
didn't just go there on Sundays which was anyway a social thing
and done everywhere, but on Wednesday nights as well and sometimes in between to help mow the grass or paint Sunday School
rooms. Asheville was a joke and the fact that he came from there
made him ridiculous, too. Nobody took Asheville seriously—that
is, if they'd even heard of it. "Nashville?" most of the guys asked
him. "The music place?"

Home was best forgotten, and Danny almost succeeded in eras-
ing from his mind the hilly streets and sudden tall frame houses,
tobacco fields tucked against blue slopes, and tang of a mountain

apple. Then he'd stepped from the Trailways at spring break and breathed in balmy air and the place rushed back to him in a flood of associations—wisps of clouds drifting across a mountain peak, the race of shadow down a green-sided gap, his grandmother calling out across her garden, "I will lift mine eyes unto the hills," and he, so much younger, knowing exactly which hills she was talking about. His hills. But you couldn't build your life on a place. That was too simple a solution. He was supposed to go somewhere, be somebody. He had to go on.

He didn't think the other guys were torn apart by where they came from. It didn't seem like they even thought about their families unless it was a football weekend and one or another of their parents came up for the game. He'd watched Ham slip so easily into the role of host, welcoming his mother who had her son's air of knowing, of being right, as she stepped from the short dark car in her navy blazer and brilliant skirt, jingling gold bracelets, smoothing sleek hair with year-round tanned hands. Ham's father slammed the car door as though emphasizing his arrival, hitching up, as he strode around the car to shake hands with his son, week-end slacks which glowed lime green like something off a kindergarten wall. Danny usually managed to skirt the parental cars lined up beside the dormitories by ducking in the back way. But the very halls of his dorm warned of the intrusion: doors were left open and the common room smelled of perfume and sacks of gift apples. Women—mothers and an occasional self-conscious older sister—wandered up and down looking for a bathroom. He brushed past, avoiding their eyes. If he ever found one of them up in the fourth floor bathroom, by god, he'd go ahead and pee anyway.

It wasn't the way they looked that bothered him, those women. His mother wore a different outfit every day and couldn't serve breakfast without her lipstick on. It was that there wasn't any awkwardness between them; after the parents left, having driven their boy out to dine in one of the tiny unadvertised restaurants in the country, the guys were neither exalted nor depressed. They accepted the visits as they accepted their parents, affectionately but without much concentration. They were, Danny decided, part of each other's lives, each part harmonizing with but not dominating the rest. So that together or apart they had an orderliness and a cer-

tainty like beautifully cared-for furniture which had been polished
by the same maid using the same rag for decades. While he rattled
around like an apple in a wheelbarrow.

He couldn't do anything about it. He couldn't change what he
came from and he couldn't change himself. He was powerless, he
had always been powerless; lacking power, you lack everything.
Funny, Danny thought, and shifted slightly in the bed so that he
could stare out the single uncurtained window at the dark opaque
nothing beyond, funny how there were the same little struggles
for supremacy going on at school as there were at home, nasty
little struggles. His father ignoring the dinner schedule; his mother
burning the roast. The headmaster, oh, very subtly put down one
of the faculty in assembly. You wouldn't have noticed if you weren't
alert. Mr. Neilson led Ham on and on in class discussion while the
other guys listened for the inevitable, and sure enough Ham fell
flat on his face and admitted that he hadn't even started reading
Macbeth. When Ham confessed, there was a tiny glint of satisfaction
in Mr. Neilson's eye. Yet there was a certain honor in being one of
Neilson's victims. It meant that at least you were important enough
to be noticed. Proof that you were one of the elite: intelligent,
and so in danger of being trapped by your vanity. Danny knew he
would never qualify for being hounded that way. But neither was
he a loser like the guys from the midwest who breathed through
their mouths, the ones Neilson badgered at the rate of one per
class just to make sure they stayed awake. No, he was in the middle somewhere, invisible to all. What he thought didn't matter to
anybody, what he'd figured out by years of watching battles from
his outpost of invisibility. Any more than it mattered to anyone
the particular misery he felt on the train coming north to school,
when he was neither one place nor the other, no longer caught
in the loneliness of home, not yet embedded in the isolation of
school. Once settled in, of course, he could claim a share in the
general student anguish over papers and early morning classes,
could blend his misery in with the crowd's complaints, the way at
home he played the much-put-upon-older-son, as if that were all
there was wrong.

He ought to force himself to get involved. He ought to have
some kind of rehearsal or study group or student council meeting

to dash off to as soon as he had eaten dinner so he would not every evening have to live through again the moment when the cafeteria was undeniably emptied of its finest and talk dipped and dulled and petered out and the only faculty left in their corner were those who for their own reasons avoided going home or who were on duty till seven, when the lights grew garish against the deep night fallen beyond the great windows, and the kitchen crew sneaked out of the steamroom to draw a cup of coffee or pick at a left-over plate of cake. The more impatient of the Irish kitchen ladies would start mopping tables. Then he had to recognize all over again that he had nothing to do but walk across the wide carpeted floor and out into the sudden clean air through cold that left him hungry for something he couldn't define, across the dark campus where only a few lights shone, most of the guys being in the library or music building across the road, or gathered in one of the smoke-filled meeting rooms where they plotted the council election. He walked up to his room to open his books and pretend he was studying. Saturday nights were the worst, tables half-empty because of guys gone home or out to dinner with their folks, those who remained clustered together in unaccustomed weekend camaraderie talking about the Woody Allen film playing on campus that night and how they would fill in the hours before it began. The school never arranged for any more entertainment than that after the time they had paid for some lah-de-dah quartet from the city and only three guys and a handful of teachers showed up for the concert. He kept forgetting to tell Aunt Mae about that; she would have loved the expression on the musicians' faces when they walked out onto the assembly hall stage and realized that almost every seat was empty. They sat down and played, anyway, which he thought was pretty gutsy. They were all right, but he'd rather listen to his aunt play.

Far below, the heavy back door slammed, the sound echoing up the stairwell. Some of the guys must have ordered out for pizza, though it was strictly forbidden to open that door after ten p.m. Most likely Tim Dewar and his crowd; they would graduate having broken every rule in the book. More power to them if they could get away with it. Supper must have been the usual lousy Saturday leftovers from the week before. You had to order out for pizza just to survive. He'd skipped the meal altogether to work on his history paper. Danny got out of bed and went to his desk where his notebook and copy of The Federalist Papers were arranged in perfect parallel position beneath the lamp. He switched the light on. He didn't have a first paragraph written yet. He didn't even have a first sentence. He had to write the damn thing before Monday and he had to do a good job. His father was a historian, for christ's sake; he spent most of his life sitting in his office spinning out junk like this. There was for sure something wrong with him if he couldn't write a five page history paper for Slim Jim Masterson who was so dumb that he must have gotten his nickname not for his incredible skinniness, but for the fact that you could chew and chew over what he said in class and every time get nothing but a mouthful of junk.

If he stayed up all night he could write the first draft, then type it after chapel tomorrow and still have time to do the rest of his reading. If he didn't write it, he would flunk the course. Then his father would kill him. He would get right on the phone and lecture him about wasting this great opportunity to get an education and if he didn't straighten up and fly right and make something of himself, they would pull him out and send him to military school. Did Danny want to spend the next year and a half of his life learning to polish a rifle and salute? Danny, if his father really wanted to know, didn't much care what he learned in the next year and a half, but he wasn't about to tell Danny's father that. It only prolonged the lecture. Danny had learned long ago that the best way to keep his sanity at home was to keep his mouth shut. And, whatever they expected him to do, to do the opposite. When his mom called him away from the basketball court in the middle of a pickup game to come and speak graciously to her friends, he walked down the driveway as slowly as humanly possible and didn't drop his scowl until he was within arm's reach. He always straightened out his expression then. If too provoked, his mother might well put her arms around him and stroke his shoulder in that extra gentle way, thus trapping him until she had finished her conversation. Her voice would become vaguely tearful: "This is Danny, my oldest. He goes away to school now, so I only get him on vacations." She allowed no hint in her tone that he had turned out to be a bit more trouble than they had bargained for.

They had never given him time, room, to work out what he was or wasn't. To them he was one more Pearson possession to be kept in proper working order. This kept him, at home, in a continual mood of rebellion against their expectations. Even the kid, Nathan, expected something of him. It made him feel guilty all the time; even if he wasn't consciously breaking one of their rules, he felt like he was somehow letting someone down. He couldn't work out exactly what it was they wanted of him. But he felt like whatever he did, whatever he became, they were going to be disappointed. He would never be quite enough. He ought to be relieved that they'd sent him away, to a school where no one particularly cared or noticed what he did as long as he made it to class on time and answered a few questions and handed in some kind of work. But with nothing to react against, he felt like a jar of marshmallow fluff from which the jar has been removed—a formless, purposeless blob. At home, they saw him as a reflection of their own desires. Here, he was invisible. Every muscle in his face ached with the effort of figuring out what he ought to do. But what did it matter what he did since he didn't really exist? With his pen he drew great black gashes across his empty paper.

On the night of the university orchestra's rehearsal, Mae hesitated at the open double doors, letting a group of brass players push past her. "How are ya!" they shouted to Jason Dewar as if calling across a football stadium. He raised one hand to them, then bent back over the score which was spread on the wide black conductor's stand. Abandoning their instruments on a table in the far corner, the brass players regrouped around the jowly man who had been in the middle of a long anecdote as Mae followed them in from the vestibule. No one else had arrived. It was going to be hard to cross that wide floor towards the empty half-circle of chairs, Jason Dewar perched above on his tall stool.

Mae hugged her violin case to her chest. It was like walking into her first audition. Except that she had already met the judge and more than half suspected that she wouldn't live up to his expectations. She stood very straight and still; if she slipped quickly back to the hall, she could get home and finish re-fingering the partita she wanted to learn. Andy could tell Jason Dewar that she'd changed her mind. She should have waited in the bathroom until more of the orchestra had gotten here and then walked in behind them. She gasped; without realizing it she had been holding her breath like a child courting invisibility. She had to disappear before Jason Dewar indicated by some word or look that he remembered that she was the one who had telephoned him in the middle of the night.

He looked up from his music then, right at her. She could al-

most hear him remembering, but he simply jerked his chin as if
to say "come on in, then." She made herself walk towards him,
cringing at each sharp tap of her heels.

"I'm glad you decided you could join us after all." He studied
her over a pair of half-lensed reading glasses. The eraser end of his
pencil continued to beat against the metal stand as if he was unwilling to completely interrupt the pulse of the music he concentrated
on.

"Well, Andy kept fussing at me to expand my professional hori-
zons." She spoke ironically, but either the name or the irony es-
caped him, for he simply stared at her a moment longer and turned
back to his score. In the fluorescent light of the rehearsal room,
the grey in his dark hair stood out like notes on a page.

"Where would you like me to sit?" Her voice deepened in embarrassment. She disliked interrupting him for such a trivial matter,
but she couldn't just go on standing there until the other players had all arrived and claimed their chairs and she had located
the empty place and finally sat, new child in the schoolroom.
She needed somewhere to settle in this vast indifferent hall which
smelled of stale cigarettes and the cold metal of folding chairs dusty
from a summer in storage.

He raised his head, but kept his eyes on the hand which pen-
cilled notes on the score. "Until the section leaders give me their
final decisions, I'll have to ask you to sit third stand, inside chair.
That's Mrs. Finney's old place, so no one will be offended if you
take it. Unless you are, of course." He gave her his full attention
then, his tone speculative. "Do you mind sitting so far back?"

"Of course not!" Mae's laugh crescendoed, then circled in on
itself and broke. Imagine Jason Dewar taking the time to worry
over such a thing—and so she laughed—or Mae Cavin—but as she
listened to her overly-loud denial and first snort of laughter, she
grew more embarrassed and her laugh more forced. "That will be
fine, Mr. Dewar; thank you." She turned, pushing two chairs out
of her way without bothering to realign them. So he thought it
was her ego which made her reluctant to join his little ensemble,
vanity which made her protest against losing her own voice to the
noise of this group. As if rank among these musicians amounted
to a hill of beans. Well, she was here because Andy thought it was

important, but she would stay only if she could retain her sense
of distance. She would not allow even this so-great conductor to
make her feel like one inconsequential part of his whole. She was
Mae Cavin, first violinist of the Back Street Quartet. Mae found her
chair and unpacked her violin, leaving the case open across her
lap. She played scales to herself until her fingers had reclaimed
her thoughts, bending her head to hear better, her ear almost flat
against the wood, her eyes closed.

But the room was filling with sound: quick blats of a horn, the
lush trickle of a clarinet down a scale, the click of cases opened and
shoved away on metal tables, the hushed scratch of rosin against
bows. And over it all, creeping between Mae and the lackadaisical
melody she was making up as another sort of artist might doodle,
fingers loose around a stub of pencil, to pass the time, over it all
the buzz of conversations begun outside and trapped now in the
rehearsal hall, words bouncing and re-echoing around walls built
to hold music in from the rest of the department.

The players moved slowly towards their chairs, walking two by
two or in small groups made up of every instrument, not splitting
apart until they reached Jason's podium and had to divide into their
proper sections. Even then they lingered, holding one another up
with talk until every member of the section had arrived, so that
they all sat down together as if on cue. A short heavy-set man with
the puckish grin of a spoiled child momentarily contented stood
before the chair next to Mae's, shouting something to a cellist. He
gave Mae the briefest of nods and sat, plunging into the opening
notes of the Bruch concerto before stopping to lean forward, violin
and bow dangling between his wide knees, and yell to his friend:
"You didn't tell me what her name was."

Jason never looked up. But when the seats had filled and the
concertmaster had gestured to the oboe for the "a" and they had
tuned, winds and brass and strings and then all together, then,
some ten minutes after they should have begun, which Mae endured by sitting with her back several rigid inches from the back
of her chair and trying not to think of the partita she might have
learned at home, then, Jason clapped his hands twice and pulled
off his reading glasses. The scurries of sound stopped at once. Mae
pictured the scene as written: "Crowd: freeze; spotlight and all

eyes center front on raised figure."

"Good evening." One of the brass players called back, "Hello!" Jason ignored him. "As you all know one another intimately by this time and as you all, I trust, have heard at least enough gossip to know that I am Jason Dewar and here to take charge of the university's orchestral program for the year while the department looks for someone to replace Dr. Finney, we'll get right to the business of the evening."

The musicians were murmuring with laughter, awaiting his next remarks when he raised his arms. "Brahms 3rd, first movement." He gave them thirty seconds. There was a unison frantic groping through folders. He lifted his right hand a fraction, held it there, dropped it. Most were somewhere near the right note after the first few bars.

He stopped them at once. "I know it's the first time through but please. Winds, you can find those pitches if you try." They played four lines and he stopped them again. "Strings, you're dragging. You've got to watch me. Again." He tapped his stick sharply on his stand. Mae's stand partner was shuffling his feet. The third time Jason Dewar stopped them, he dropped his arms and stepped back to look around. The orchestra waited, instruments still ready, but as he stood without speaking, they wilted back in their chairs, pulling their instruments to their laps.

"I don't know what Dr. Finney's method of rehearsing you was," he began. No, Mae thought. Don't do that. "I did hear you play a concert under him when I visited in the spring. I was quite impressed. In fact, that's one of the reasons I accepted the position. I was quite impressed but not completely impressed. I heard rough edges that ought to have been eliminated in the earliest rehearsals, would have been, if you had given the music your complete, undivided attention. While you play under me, I expect just such attention. At the first rehearsal and at the concert. Tonight, before we break at ten, I expect to hear the quality of music that you might offer to an audience, even if you manage only a moment's worth."

No head nodded in response; no one met his eyes. There was merely the mute raising of instruments as they obeyed his lifted arms. The faces around Mae were blank, closed against the conductor's tardy gesture of companionship. "I know we can do it.

Come: Brahms from the beginning." In that moment Mae felt stir the oldest of female instincts, the urge to take care of one more vulnerable then herself.

The three hours dragged by. Whenever Mae felt the music swell within, around her, pure sound binding her to these nameless players, compelling her for that instant to share everything, music, friendship, time, in their mutual attempt to satisfy the man who led, he stopped them, skipped them ahead or back and once right over the rest of a movement as if it had never been written. "Fine. Fauré."

He complimented the winds once, and nodded when the percussion achieved a beautifully muted drum roll, but never in the evening did he hint at his love for the music or for those who made it. Mae pitied him; he had no idea how merciless the group might be. Even now, as they played for him, they were comparing him to their dear old Dr. Finney, who had joked and jollied them through rehearsals. Mae sent him mental messages as she played, she warned him to keep tighter control of his mouth when the bassoon missed an entrance for the second time. You can't frown every time; you have to let them relax a little. Give them some sign that they're as important to you as the quality of the pianissimo. Even if they're not. They won't take your criticism otherwise. They're used to gentler handling. They're like children. But there was nothing she could do for him. As leader, he would be allowed no miscalculation, no faulty strategy. Technically there was no chance of that; he was master of his art. But he expected too much of them. He let them know every time when they let him down. They wouldn't easily forgive him that.

She didn't like the way he ran rehearsal, either, but not because she would have preferred Dr. Finney. She would resist anyone who told her when to play and how. She had used too many years learning to decide for herself how a piece ought to sound, learning to assert her own interpretation over that of her teachers. It had been painful, breaking from their authority. She couldn't, now, give in and rely on someone else's judgment.

Yet she couldn't rebel now, couldn't walk out on the rehearsal. Jason would lump her with the rest of those unable to accept professional criticism. Already he expected her to act like a prima donna.

At the break she rushed outside. The shock of the chill air calmed her, reminded her of her existence beyond this emotional battle of follow-the-leader.

"He's a bastard." A man spoke behind her as the door crashed shut. There was the scrape and flare of a match and the pungent tang of cigarette. "He runs rehearsal like we were a high school band he has to order around. I wonder if he'll stick out the year."

"Or if we stick out the year with him." Mae recognized the emphatic voice of her stand partner.

"Hah. I'm not sure how long I can put up with someone telling me how to phrase every measure. But don't sweat it, he'll end up going back to the glitzy audiences and the big bucks. Like the rest of the hot-shot names, stepping on our minor musician necks to get where they want to be."

"He'll think twice before climbing on my neck." Her stand partner laughed, an ugly short burst of sound. "What I don't understand is what he's doing down here in the first place. He obviously didn't come for love of us." Mae moved to the end of the wide porch, away from the light, and looked up at the trees which screened the music building from the rest of the campus. Her stand partner sat on the low railing, kicking his feet against the stone as he talked. Smoke from the cellist's cigarette spread out into the night.

"Well," he finally said, in a voice as indistinct and purposeless as the smoke, "they say he needed a rest. He directed his orchestra full time and was also running around to fill guest slots all over the country. I think the only place he wasn't wanted was with his wife." The two broke into laughter, then bent their heads to continue in lower tones. Mae moved down the steps to the dirt path which wound around the building. She didn't want to hear any more. Jason Dewar had to expect gossip; he was fair game. A man of his stature must be used to having them take his past for fodder. What disturbed her was their complaint of his work. Such angry talk, even if forgotten as soon as spoken, would build him the reputation of exactly what people wanted to believe artists were. Selfish, tyrannical, insensitive. More than likely, Mae admitted, he was; certainly he was gruff where he might be gentle, sarcastic, where he might praise. But she was beginning to believe he had a heart. No one could hear music as he did and share what he heard in such a way that he could move a group of fairly average musicians to hear it also and even to approach playing what they heard, no man could do all that and have no sensitivity. But he would have no opportunity to prove it to them if they all decided tonight that they wouldn't work for him.

A narrow door at the side of the building was unlocked. Pushing it open, Mae stepped into the basement hallway. Up and down as far as she could see, practice rooms lined the corridor; most with doors gaping open and dark at this hour, a few revealing by the line of light against the floor that someone inside still worked. None was larger than a few square feet, room only for a battered upright practice piano and a music stand. They were cells, really, where each student faced alone the test of whether or not he had it, the gift. Not just a good ear or deep feeling and the yen to express it. But discipline, bound with such desire for music that he would accept living in a windowless corridor like a submarine's, spending hours every day in an airless cubicle with buzzing fluorescent lights where time of day and weather never changed, emerging at the end exhausted, startled by the fresh air and variations in light. Yet he would walk home across the shadow-dappled campus triumphant, filled with the joy of having worked hard all day at what he was meant to do.

She had spent hours in a cell like this one. Solitary as a monk; no, more so. Surely, a monk retreated to his solitude to speak to a God he at least suspected might hear him. While she had played hour after hour to herself, scales and those damned arpeggios and exercises until her fingers were raw and her neck ached, with only a vague, wistful hope that she was in the right profession. She'd had no liturgy to assure her that she wasn't deluding herself, dreaming up some fantastical ideal. No one welcomed her in, assured her that she had attained her goal or even that there was a goal for her to attain. Yes, you will be a musician, dear. We're glad you've decided to be one of us. The prayers she would have prayed if someone might even have hinted that! Yes, of course you can make a living at this. She would have been overjoyed with any gleam of assurance to rekindle her faith, would have worked three times as hard. Her teacher, Professor Leon, had instructed her only in technique. The precise placement of a finger, the slant of the left wrist. How to produce the fullest tone. And always, always, how to try to hear the sound that Beethoven or Lalo or the great Mozart had heard when he composed the piece. Professor Leon might have known each of the composers personally, so certain was he of how a phrase must be played. As certain as he was in the pronunciation of their names. There was no slurring there. The syllables came cleanly, even exaggerated with a click of old teeth: Mots-zart. Never, slurred, Mo-zart. He knew. After an hour with him, Mae was sure that she knew nothing. She walked to her room drained and terrified. She had no profession. She would have no career. She had no hope of being a musician.

But for some reason, she had kept on practicing. She couldn't remember now how she had been able to keep at it. Not enough imagination to figure out what else to do, probably, as well as an obstinate refusal to have her family pity her for lack of talent. Then, once, had come the briefest suggestion of comradeship: Professor Leon had placed a hand on her shoulder after a lesson and joked with her. She had played Beethoven for him, one of the Romances; he had been pleased. His stumpy fingers gripped the bone of her shoulder as they stood together at the door of his studio. For a moment it was as though a great eagle had alighted there. She felt a surge of joy at this trust. Then his short thick hand was again sketching in the air the proper shape of a phrase. Those hands; when she was first brought to him she had doubted that he was any kind of a violinist. He should have had long, graceful hands, with tapering fingers. But she had been so stupid, full of misty ideas about what a musician's life must be like. Professor Leon wiped those clouds away. He had been fierce with her, relentless. It was because of him that she loved the Degas print of the stout dancing master and still practiced before it. She could hear him shout at the girl bent over the barre, "Off! Off! Your rhythm is all off! This is an art that requires you to have a mind! I assume you have one in there somewhere. Think! Think it out for yourself. Don't wait for me to tell you. Don't hypnotize yourself with sound."

Every step of this corridor made her relive that struggle for belief. It swelled from the beige-bland walls, the desire of young ones yearning for a future. It transfigured each rush of sound from the occupied rooms—the piano hurrying up and down the scale, the clarinet's muddled arpeggios—an endless regimen repeated again in another musician's search for discipline.

"I always thought," she told Danny during her visit last spring, "I always thought that if only I knew I was a musician, nothing else would ever be difficult. If I could just have that one thing and be sure about it, I could handle anything that came along. My whole life would just fall into place. But it doesn't happen like that, Danny. I was doing all the things a musician does, yet I was still the same old me, worried about whether or not I really was part of the profession. I still had all my old mean petty habits: I hated talking to anyone in the morning, I made fun of people I didn't know. I guess I had this idea that being a musician would be as certain a thing as the fiery bush that Moses saw, that it would be something I would have no doubts about, and so all-consuming that it would make me forget the normal drudgery of living. But life doesn't work like that." Danny had listened in silence, then shrugged his shoulders before he answered in a flat voice, "Well, I don't have anything like that, anyway."

Mae climbed back to the first floor, her steps muffled by the cement tread of the stairs. At the landing, she paused; the noise from below was cut off as though a heavy door had slammed shut. She could hear the burr of the drinking fountain outside the rehearsal room as she hurried up the last steps. It was then, if she had to pinpoint the moment, that her instinctual reaction to the evening seeped through to her conscious mind with such accumulated force that she finally recognized it as an inclination whch demanded action. The process might be called making a decision if it had occurred more logically, if it were less tangled with her emotions, and if the instinct had emerged more firmly bound with a tangible deed. She would stay with the orchestra in case Jason Dewar needed her support. Not, she thought as she again took her chair and watched the musicians drifting into place with more reluctance than earlier, not that she had evidence that he would want her help. But she had lived so long on instinct—she'd had nothing else, really, all these years, unless you counted Andy's help —that she automatically obeyed this one. She would remain on the sidelines, but she would keep an eye on him. With that resolve, Mae threw herself into the rest of the rehearsal, fully alert to every nuance of his expression. Alert, also, to the mood of the orchestra as it submitted to his corrections. Perhaps to soften a scolding he gave the strings, he did tell them one story. He was conducting the Boston Pops at the Hatch Shell in one of the summer concerts when a bee flew into the opened mouth of the soprano soloist just as she breathed in with all the strength of her massive chest. "She nearly died," Jason said straight-faced, "And so did we." The laughter which followed was quite real, Mae thought, not merely tolerant. So they weren't yet to the point of freezing him out with sullen silence. But they continued to watch him warily, as wild animals do a human, awaiting his next move. Jason raised his arms. "Again," he told the strings. His voice was tired. For him, Mae played her heart out, though no one would know it but the man who sat beside her, stolid, indifferent, his legs spread wide to support his body.

At ten Jason let them go, right on time though they had begun late. The players ebbed away, with none of the raucous joking with which they'd entered, except for the section leaders, who gathered in a tight circle to discuss the evening. Jason stood at their edge, his arms folded, listening to their comments as though they were not part of the group he had just badgered all evening. Mae touched his shoulder. "It wasn't so bad," she said. Then quickly, lest he feel the need to return some gracious phrase, good, good, glad you're with us, she rushed away.

Mae tried once or twice more to reach Danny. But the sense of urgency had passed. She was no longer haunted by the uneasiness of several weeks ago, and dialed his dorm number from a kind of dutiful habit, her ear meanwhile superimposing the chords of Brahms on the distant double ring of the telephone. Each time her hand circled the dial and paused to let the numbers spin back around to zero, what she saw was Jason Dewar's hand shaping rhythms in the air. When for the third or fourth time the dorm phone rang unanswered, she hung up unperturbed.

Every Monday night she went to orchestra rehearsal, and every day for the remainder of the week she raged at having to do so. It wasn't just the loss of her practice time; she could always get up earlier for that. What bothered her was starting her week off in a

crowd, sitting there for three hours among those PhD's-in-music
who took themselves so seriously. She needed time to herself to re-
cover from the students who demanded her welcome and advice,
and to prepare for the next day's batch. That was the drawback to
teaching at home; she was at the mercy of any student who chose
to come early, catching her with her hair uncombed. Then there
were those, more numerous, who arrived late. "I can always practice," she reassured those who apologized. Yes, but she was still
aware of the waiting, of her own life suspended, of planning out
the lesson ahead. She needed any nights that the quartet didn't
perform to stretch out in. She needed to recreate that sense of contented solitude. She needed emptiness, with the assurance that at
midnight, Andy would call. But now, when she was alone, faces
from the orchestra turned on her; their whispers thrust through
her thoughts. In the midst of working to get a trill absolutely even
she found herself wondering whether Lem and his cellist friend
would quit the orchestra. Lem's eyebrows were black and thick,
growing across the bridge of his nose. The one time he had spoken
directly to her, they seemed to bristle with disdain.

"So, you're enjoying your new career with us?" The sarcasm
in his voice was surely her imagination. He had no reason to be
antagonistic, unless he guessed her distaste for him; an idea which
was no more unreasonable than the thought which came later;
sending embarrassment flaring through her, that he had guessed
that her arrival had much to do with Jason Dewar.

"Figure it out on your own if you don't like the way I've fingered
it for you," she snapped at her favorite student, a thin, intense
boy she'd tried for two years to win from timidity. He seemed to
disappear beneath the curtain of limp, colorless hair which hung
before his eyes. "What I mean is," she said more quietly, "if you
find a fingering which is easier for you than what I've suggested,
go ahead and write it down. Don't leave it to chance and come up
with something different every time you play this."

"O.K." Kenneth was the most gifted of her students, and she'd
let him know her excitement over his talent. Yet he continued
to slink into her studio with his wide shoulders sideways as if to
diminish his presence. Never quite certain about whether or not
he should close the door, he usually left it a careful inch or so

open. "He's never called me by name," she reported to Andy, who had retorted, "How can he? He can't call you Mae. That would be too embarrassing. He's seventeen. And 'Miss Cavin' sounds like an aging schoolteacher with stumpy legs."

"You ought to hear him. He's got such authority in his playing. When he starts a piece, he's a different person. He even stands up straight. Then the minute he stops, he slumps back into himself again."

Kenneth's hands, she noticed as he stuffed his music into a patched green knapsack, his hands were scrubbed clean as a surgeon's. Jason's hands were like that. "Your music will last longer if you're a little easier on it."

"I know," he said, and walked out, almost closing the door behind him.

He's not being rude, she reminded herself, leaning on the piano to await her next student. That's just the way he is, absorbed in something going on in his head. Jason Dewar probably walked around like that. And as her next student, Melissa Wilkins, bounced in, flipping her sandy hair back over one shoulder and demanding to start work on the Mozart her mother had bought for her, Mae wondered what Jason Dewar had been thinking about in the long silence which had followed the orchestra's first complete run-through of the Brahms last week. He had leaned back on the conductor's stool, his eyes closed, his head tipped to the ceiling as though he were listening to the echo of the final bars. It took her a moment to tune in to Melissa's petulant, "But why not?" and to assume the brisk, extra-loud voice with which she bustled the girl away from her mother's fantasies of a prodigy.

By the weekend, Mae was in control again, the intruding faces dimmed. But with the next Monday, tension mounted in her like the rush of nerves through the orchestra when Jason raised his arms, held them all at the ready while he took a quick survey of his players, then plunged into the downbeat. Bow poised on the string, wrist aching with the urge to begin, Mae felt in that long moment of waiting for the downbeat all the anxiety which surely made him hesitate to drop his arms: what if they don't come in, come in late, come in timidly?

Mae slipped into rehearsals speaking to no one, careful to ar-rive after the hall was filled with musicians loudly greeting one another. At the break she went out the side door and paced up and down beneath the night-black trees until the silence on the smoking porch alerted her that it was time to go in. If Andy knew how she hurried, head down, back to her seat, dodging all conversation, he would be incredulous. Already he wanted to know who she talked with, what she'd found out about who was playing where and for how much. Mae smiled up at the large clock on the cement block wall. She was receiving none of the benefits with which they had persuaded her to join the orchestra. Jason Dewar had never recalled his promise to give her some university students. But, and Mae tried to pinch her smile back to sobriety, but she got to watch Jason Dewar.

He stood three stands away, eyes dropping to his score, then around to his players, quick to catch any flutter of uneasiness that indicated a player was lost and needed help, giving a nod of "well-done" if the player recovered himself on his own. Watching them all, noting what had gone wrong, with scarcely a breath between his impatient tap on the stand to stop them—"No, No, NO"—and the curt announcement of where they would begin—"Measure 213"—and his eyes seemed to be everywhere. Mae felt, rather than saw, his look at her. She was absorbed in counting out a difficult syncopated passage, yet she knew he was watching her. When she looked up a few bars later, glancing up for the beat, he had turned away. Yet whenever he cued the violins, it was her he looked at. She was sure of it. He was never still, his eyes darted to the brass section while his hands cued in the cellos; he twisted his body back to the main body of the orchestra and then rose on his toes to reach towards the double basses. He was with them before the music came and moved along as they played it, living in anticipation of the next beat, next measure, hearing whole phrases before they were played. Then he looked at Mae and there was a shock of stillness within the surge of sound.

After the rehearsal he was surrounded by infatuated music students who had come to observe, ignoring their teachers' less-than-favorable comments about the great conductor. Around Mr. Dewar, the girls became bold and pushed forward in the circle formed around him to ask questions. The boys stood with folded arms, their faces agitated in silent pleas for attention. Jason Dewar was gravely courteous to them all. Mae waited on the edge of the circle until the last student had finished his suggestion of how the Brahms ought to be played, based on his study of someone's recording, then brushed past her with the bright scent of shampoo.

"I'm afraid I have to miss next week's rehearsal," she said to Jason Dewar. "We're doing the last of our Schubert series at the library. We scheduled them last spring. I don't mean to weasel out of your rehearsal."

"Surely it's your rehearsal, too, Miss Cavin?" He looked at her coolly. "But do whatever you have to do. Our first concert is in three weeks."

She turned away before she apologized again, raging at him for making her feel irresponsible.

Andy's feet, in low black boots, hung over one end of the sofa. His head was propped on a stack of throw pillows Mae had arranged—print, solid blue, print—just before he arrived, forgetting his propensity to transform his surroundings into a chaotic comfort.

"You're no help at all," she hurled at him. "You haven't listened to a thing I've said these past weeks. All this is tying me up in knots."

Andy raised his head and held it awkwardly to look at Mae on the rug below. "You're being dramatic again." He let his head drop back to the pillows. "If playing with that orchestra once a week is really such a torture, then quit. It's that simple. It's not like you've signed a contract, for god's sake. They're a small university ensemble, not the New York Philharmonic."

"I can't just walk out on them." Mae hesitated before the last word. Then, embarrassed that Andy might guess what she had almost said, she threw scorn across the low glass coffeetable. "So now you're calling it a charming little ensemble. A month ago you made it sound like god's gift to the orchestral world."

"It was your decision to join, Mae. But if you can't live with it, tell Jason your schedule is too full and drop out."

"Just like that."

"Why not? You don't have a personal obligation to anyone at the university." Andy laid a hand against the back of her neck. "Calm down, Mae. I'm not going to fight with you over this. I'm trying to help you sort it out. Just be reasonable. If you don't like it, then you need to decide to do something different. Quit. Or, if you decide to stick with it, convince yourself that it's worthwhile. You don't want to spend the whole fall agonizing over this. I know I don't want to spend it listening to you complain about rehearsals."

"I'm not complaining about the rehearsals." Mae stopped, and tried again. "Whatever happened to the students the two of you promised? I haven't heard a word about them since I agreed to join the orchestra."

"Why don't you ask Jason?" Andy asked quietly, flexing the fingers of his left hand.

"Why should I have to beg for something that was part of an agreement?" Mae was up now, pacing between the table and the couch. "Why should I have to get down on my knees and crawl to the great Jason Dewar when I've fulfilled my part of the bargain? Why should I get stuck in the part of the nagging female?" She stuffed the remains of their deli supper into the white sack, noting that she was the one, as usual, to do the cleaning up. "You men, you're so bloody conceited. It's just like you always do. Say anything, pull out the sweet-talk, so you can get what you want, then skip blithely on ahead without taking a bit of responsibility." She whirled around from the trash can. "It's not funny!"

Choking, Andy sat up. "I'm sorry. I hear what you're saying and I'm not laughing at you. It's just the idea of Jason Dewar sweet-talking anyone." He reached blindly for his cold drink and knocked over the cup. Listening to his apologies and mopping ice from the table quieted Mae. He did his best, she thought. She couldn't expect him to understand her when she hadn't told him everything.

Andy pulled her down on the couch beside him. "You told me after that first rehearsal that you thought Jason would have problems with the department. Remember? Well, you were right. He's really struggling to get enough power just to accomplish the most basic things. So many of the faculty are resisting him that he's paralyzed."

"But why?" Mae breathed; although she knew well enough why. It was fulfillment to hear someone talk about Jason Dewar.

"His way of doing things is a bit abrasive, I guess." Andy

shrugged. "Maybe you've noticed. Anyway, they criticize the music
he selects, they pick at the way he runs his workshops for student
conductors. I doubt they'd let him near the schedule, let alone the
placement of students with teachers. I have a feeling that the reason
you haven't heard anything more about those students we talked
about is that he's not able to arrange them for you."

"How do you know?" Mae demanded.

"My dear, you may despise the notion of talking with the musicians of the academic world, but I have friends among them."

"Well, why didn't he just tell me? Instead of letting me think
he'd broken his promise."

"I imagine he would rather that you thought him forgetful than
have to admit to you that he doesn't have the authority he's supposed to have."

"That's absurd."

"That's the way with the rich and famous. It's only to us little
drudges that details like professional courtesy have earthshaking
meaning."

"So what am I supposed to do in the meantime?" Mae asked,
but her voice had long since lost its stridency.

"Do what you want to do."

"Andy, you'd say that if we were going down with the Titanic."

He smiled and reached for her hand. "I expect it would apply
all the more, then."

"I'm glad I've got you," Mae said impulsively, taken, at the touch
of his hand, back to the evening their friendship had been decided.
Andy's hand gripped hers more firmly; he must remember, also.
It had been about a year after they first met at his daughter's recital. They had driven for hours along fall-bright back roads to a
town in western Massachusetts where the quartet was to play in the
high school auditorium. At the reception following the concert,
the president of the local women's club had embraced the four of
them. She talked at length of the problems of creating culture so
far from the city, while Andy finished off several saucers-worth of
toothpicked meatballs and cubed orange cheeses. Eventually she
interrupted herself and departed, bearing with her the coats and
hats and music of the Gardeners. The Gardeners, instruments in
hand, followed meekly behind, to be introduced to the club mem-

ber who would house them for the night. She returned clasping
the arm of a small round woman who smiled brightly at Mae. "I'll
be your hostess tonight," she said. "Wasn't it a lovely concert! You
all play so well." She patted Mae's hand between her own. "I know
you must be tired after working so hard. Let me take you home.
You, too," she carolled over her shoulder to Andy, who lingered
beside the meatball tureen. She talked at them continuously as the
aging Volkswagen chugged around several miles of curves, but as
she had insisted the two of them sit together in the back seat, they
heard very little of what she said until she drew up before a tall
brick farmhouse. "And I got the house," she concluded. "I've put
you on the top floor. Now if there's anything you need, anything at
all, you only have to ask. I'm right down the stairs." She left them
with promises of a tray of coffee in the morning. Two flights below,
her voice rose faintly to them. "I'll leave the two of you to yourselves now. Good night." Only then did Mae realize the woman's
mistake.

Andy stood behind a rocking chair, rocking it absently back and
forth with the tips of his fingers. The ceiling beside him slanted
sharply down to the plank floor, the four windows set in deep
alcoves. Ruffled rose curtains were tied back beneath flounced
valences. "It's a lovely room," Mae offered.

"It's a little girl's room." He nodded towards the low bookshelves. *Black Beauty, Little Women, Jane Eyre,* Mae read, with a pang of
nostalgia. The rocking chair squeaked on the polished floor. Mae
moved to a window and stared out at the moonlight which seemed
to warm the rolling fields below. Thin clouds scudded across the
sky. "It's awfully quiet," Mae said. "I can't believe we were in the
city just a few hours ago." The clouds ran over the great yellow
moon, making shadows dance on the lawn. Andy stepped behind
her. The wool of his green sweater was rough against her arm as he
raised his to point to a distant glimmer. "That might be Boston,"
he said. "All those frantic people reduced to a scattering of lights
on the horizon."

"Where they belong," Mae answered, keenly aware of his breath
moving her hair. In a kind of panic, she turned; then, without in-
tending it, surely without his planning for it to happen, she stepped
into his arms which closed around her and drew her close. He

rested his chin on top of her head, then, in a movement which would alter forever the course of their relationship, bent and nuzzled her hair before taking her face between his hands. It was, Mae thought as they kissed, like curling up tight in a warm bed, to kiss someone you have known so long who knows so much of you; the kiss was companionship, was comfort, was, and she marked the change, passion, given to them by the kindly hostess who put them in the same bedroom.

Yet they had pulled away from one another (Mae's hand curled more tightly in Andy's, and he smiled down at her, almost sadly, and she was certain he also remembered). Andy's arm had remained draped over her shoulders, but self-consciously, as if to remove it or for Mae to step away was too definite a decision. They hadn't known what to do next. The obvious answer loomed before them: the wide four-poster bed where a teenaged girl had lain beneath a starched canopy to read *Wuthering Heights*. But standing there, looking at it, Mae and Andy hesitated for too long, long enough for each to acknowledge the moment as one of embarrassment rather than desire, and to recall the easy warmth their friendship had allowed which would almost certainly be spoiled by an attempt at more.

No longer shy, they giggled over the mix-up as they dressed for bed. They lay together without touching. "I'm starved," Andy had groaned. "Love always makes me hungry," which set Mae off in a torrent of laughter that shook the bed. Andy prodded her with his elbow. "Ssh. She'll hear you downstairs." The thought of their hostess lying below and looking scandalized up at her shaking ceiling left Mae flopping back and forth in helpless laughter which Andy tried to stifle by cupping one hand over her mouth. She bit him, and they wrestled in silence for a few minutes when sleep suddenly overcame Mae. She remembered hearing Andy whisper something about a good choice and nodding in agreement and, because he wouldn't be able to see her nod in the dark, clutching his hand to her chest like a favorite teddy bear.

"If you didn't storm around every now and again I would never be so appreciative of how easy my life is," Andy's voice drew her back to the present. "Your emotional crises do serve a purpose."

"Maybe you ought to hire me to come over and rage at you."

Mae wiggled away from him as the phone rang.

"Remember, we've already had our crisis for the evening," he yelled as she ran to the music room.

A crackle of static hit her ear when she picked up the phone. She jerked her head away to avoid another blow, as Danny's voice, faint and scratchy as if from an old gramophone, came over the line.

"Aunt Mae?"

She sat on the piano bench, raking a pile of xeroxed music out of her way. "Danny! How good to hear your voice! Where are you?"

"Oh, I'm at school." Did he sound a little too determinedly casual? His next words confirmed for her that he was guarding something behind that excellent screen, adolescent off-handedness. She had heard it used, had used it herself, calling out as she left the house, "I'll be back at ten, Papa," when she knew and he knew full well that her curfew was nine-thirty. But if she could just manage the perfect blend of nonchalance and confidence, he might not notice what she was really doing—"I just thought I'd give you a call and find out how things were going in the music business," Danny said.

For the moment she allowed him the question at face value. "The quartet is doing well," she began, and knew she was talking to herself; the sentence took on that flat, inward quality of words curled back on themselves for lack of audience. There was the crash of a door against a wall, then Danny whispering. "Hey, guys, back off. I can't hear myself think in here." "Since when do you have to think to talk?" someone asked in a nasal Connecticut twang. Several voices rumbled in laughter. "Give her a kiss for me, Danno," a lighter voice put in, before disappearing in a chorus of "Way to go, Doo! Doo's doin' it!" The door crashed again.

"Sorry." Danny sounded breathless. "There's only one phone in the dorm and some of the guys get a little rowdy when they have to wait."

"It sounds like you're calling from a battlefield."

"Just about. So, how's the quartet going?"

"Pretty well, Danny. We're finishing up our Schubert series at the library and feeling proud because we've got enough society weddings scheduled through the spring to allow us all to take next summer off from performing."

"So will you get a vacation?"

"I'll still be teaching, I imagine. I'm not rich and famous enough yet to spend my summers on a yacht. By the way, one of my students is reputedly the most gorgeous girl at the high school. She's a terrible violinist, but I'd be glad to introduce you if you're coming this way on your way home and want to meet a real Yankee belle. There are some."

He laughed, though with a note of uncertainty, not old enough yet, she thought, quite to trust that she might be offering to set him up, too old to assume that she was merely teasing.

"Well, actually, that's kind of why I'm calling. I'll be off in a minute, Dewar," he hissed, in a different tone. "I was wondering if I could maybe drop by your place on the trip home. Not long, a few days or something. I'd like some time to kind of get some things straight in my mind before I have to be home."

"Of course." She spoke briskly to hide her enthusiasm. "I'm home most of the day with students, so just come on up. Or call when you get to the station and I'll meet you." She spoke as if it were all arranged; if she sounded too welcoming, he would shy away; he had Justina's almost morbid fear of creating inconvenience for others, a fear which, in his mother, often led her to concoct circuitous schemes which caused people more trouble than if she had gone ahead with her original plan.

"Oh, I can find your apartment, no problem." He sounded jubilant with relief. "Thanks a lot, Aunt Mae. I'll drop you a line right before I come down. No surprises, I promise." As he hung up, she heard him calling to the next in line. "All right, Dewar, it's yours," and the door crashed open again before she had a chance to say goodbye or ask, as she belatedly realized she ought to have done, whether his parents knew he was making his own plans for his vacation.

"It was Danny." Mae dropped onto the sofa, shoving Andy's feet aside. "He's going to stop and visit on his way home for Thanksgiving."

"Great." Andy prodded her in the side with his toes. "So why such a mean expression?"

She mock-scowled at him. "Not mean; worried. I'm wondering if I ought to call Justina and make sure they know what he's doing."

"The kid's seventeen. Give him some space. Give me some space." He beat gently against her with his legs. "Who said you could come sit on this couch anyway?"

"It's my couch, you bum." She began tickling him.

"Let go, let go." When he gasped for mercy she let him sit up.

He looked musingly at her across the safe width of the sofa. "I wonder why it is that we never got together, the two of us."

Mae felt as though a balloon suddenly inflated inside of her, creating a vacuum which denied space for her lungs to expand, her heart to beat. What on earth did he mean? He had been part of that silent decision, the choice the two of them had made before that attic window so many years ago when both pulled away at the same time from a kiss which could have gone much further, perhaps should have, but which, interrupted, had defined absolutely the terms of their friendship. As she breathed out, sensation rushed back in: she felt desolate, stripped of the assumptions on which their friendship had been based. She had tickled and teased and confided in and loved Andy, certain of their intimacy, all the more confident because they had never had to talk about that which had kept them close, their chastity. But it seemed that all of that had been her own imagination embroidering an incident which Andy had scarcely noticed. Mae felt horribly embarrassed. Did he even remember that evening? What, then, had that kiss been to him? A goodnight given to a colleague with whom one was forced, that trip, to share a comradely bed? Mae had to move away from the sofa. It was likely, then, that she had also fabricated the sensation that had passed between her and Jason Dewar in rehearsal. Mere emanation of her own desire. Was there any relationship which existed on its own, which hadn't been created, enlarged upon, by her imagination? She looked at the thin hands loosely cupped around Andy's knees. She had watched those hands for years, all told, gripping a sticky peg, forcing it to turn, plucking the string with a punitive twang. Now they seemed stranger's hands; she didn't know the mind which guided them. Mae grieved; a part of her life had vanished with his question. He was watching her with a puzzled expression; she forced herself, with a new discipline, to sit beside him, giving nothing away.

"We just never did, I guess."

Danny sat on the floor. His back was against the side of his bed. It arched where the metal frame cut into it. His arms gripped his bent knees. When he raised his head, the room had not changed. The walls were a stark white. A black and white poster of a Boston skyline hung over his desk. If he stretched his legs out straight, he could touch the wooden legs of the desk. It sat against the wall parallel with his bed. His wooden dresser was at one end of the room, a tall rectangular window at the other. Everything was exactly as his room last semester had been, and the room the semester before that, except for the green oval rug beneath the window. That had been left behind by the student who lived in here last year.

Danny stretched his neck back so his head lay on the mattress. He watched the mottled brown markings on the ceiling. They had never bothered him before. He squeezed his eyes shut, as tight as he could squeeze them, as though by pressure he could drive all thought out of his head.

Oh God, what am I going to do, what am I going to do, what am I going to do.

How long since he had sunk to the floor? Had he been repeating that phrase over and over in his head till he could hear no other sound?

Danny bent over, clutching at the damp towel around his waist as if he were going to be sick. He'd stood in the shower until he no longer felt the water strike him, but when he'd stepped back onto the bathroom floor chill as metal to his bare feet, all warmth and steam and the living stream of water gave way to the smell of toothpaste and cold clean tile. The row of white sinks gleamed at him. He'd panicked; suppose one of the other boys on his hall came in just then? It was too close to bedtime. He'd scurried to the door, then turned back to towel up a puddle of water from his shower. Their janitor mopped the floor every afternoon, then hung fresh military-gray curtains in the shower stalls. He always spoke kindly to Danny, and had once, when Danny was new, invited him home for Sunday afternoon. He'd never do that for the other boys.

I'm not like the other boys. I'm not part of them. I'm nothing, no thing. He shivered, then looked scornfully at the gooseflesh on his white, bare arms and legs. It was not only his body that was cold, numbed, dead. He'd gotten back to his room without knowing how.

He ought to dress. Danny reached under his bed and found jeans, a t-shirt, a tangle of socks. He pulled them on. They didn't warm him.

What am I going to do? The words began again, circling his mind like seagulls around refuse tossed in the sea. What am I going to do? He spoke the words out loud, and the way they rushed out shamed him. Instead of pronouncing them as individual syllables, they came out all in a rush, a kind of moan, the way a deaf-mute might speak, or someone terribly deformed who grabs your arm on a street corner and pokes his face into yours and tries to tell you something and you want to say "excuse me," and jerk away, meaning "don't touch me, go away," but you'd never say it in case the creature could understand. Danny whimpered. But he couldn't stop the words coming any more than he could stop his breathing.

A door slammed down the hall. Danny froze, huddling into himself, listening to the jingling tags on the collar of his advisor's dog. He recognized Mr. Foster's heavy flat-footed steps coming behind. Danny scrambled to his feet, looking around frantically; he had to hide. But he couldn't think why. He hadn't been doing anything. There wasn't anything to do. The jingling and the slapping sound of feet stopped. There was a loud knocking and the door to the right of Danny's rattled in response.

"Yes, sir?" It was the thin voice of one of the sophomores who lived next to him.

"Lights out, you guys. It's after ten. You know the rules, now."

"Yes, sir, sorry, sir. We were studying, sir." A desk chair screeched across the floor, and the other roommate chimed in. "Sorry, sir. Tomorrow's the big 2a math test."

"So study tomorrow." The door slammed. Danny dropped into his chair and arranged his history books across the desk as if he had been studying.

Mr. Foster knocked.

"Yes?"

"It's time, Dann-o. Lights out." The deep voice held no annoyance; everyone trusted Dann-o. Dann-o was a good guy. Mr. Foster added in a confiding tone, "After last night's little mischief, you know. Have to be a little strict with the rest of them. Don't want to lose all the seniors before they graduate."

"Right," Danny managed. "Good night, sir."

The jingling disappeared down the stairs. Danny sat at his desk, his arms spread before him covering his books.

"Of course Danny will want to be home at Thanksgiving," Justina finished. "They've been working so hard up there. What he needs is to come home and collapse."

She had called to make Danny's excuses the minute she found out about his notion of going to visit Mae. It was sweet of Mae to take his idea so seriously. It was awfully kind of her to tell him he could have a place to stay whenever he showed up, just like that. It meant a lot to him to have an aunt who was so interested in his goings-on. But he hadn't really thought it through. You know how boys are. Of course he would come straight home for Thanksgiving. All the Cavins were driving over for dinner and they were just dying to see him and hear all about his plans for next year. He wouldn't want to disappoint them. And, anyway, you know how his father is. Daniel said that what Danny needed to do was be rested up for finals when he went back to school. He would be better off if he came straight home instead of gallivanting around. Danny was just making trouble again.

"But I'd really love to have him," Mae repeated. "He'd be no trouble. I think he'd enjoy exploring the city on his own while I'm teaching, and we would have time together every evening. I'd like to see him."

"That's sweet of you," Justina said. "Of course he'd love being with you. Why don't you come stay with us? That way all of us would get a chance to see you. I've got a huge wild turkey ordered from the market and Aunt Cissie is bringing a ham. You could drive down with that friend of yours, you know, the one that plays the cello."

"Andy," Mae supplied.

"Yes. We'd just be one big family, all under the same roof. Won't that be fun!"

"That would be lovely, Jussie, but the timing is bad for me. The quartet has got two concerts that weekend. And I'll be starting Messiah rehearsals right after. Did I tell you that I was playing with the university orchestra now?"

"With that new conductor, yes, the one whose ex-wife is back in Cleveland spending all his money. I read about him, someplace."

"Jason Dewar."

"His son is at Carlton with Danny, you know. He's a real mess. But then, what would you expect from him, coming from a broken family. I think he lives on Danny's floor. I'm just thankful Danny never got mixed up with him. But, of course, Danny's got sense." Then, with scarcely a breath for transition, she asked her sister, "Is life treating you well, Mae?"

"Is life treating me well?" Mae laughed. "Whatever are you worried about that for?"

"I just wondered." She sounded hurt. "You seem like you're happy. Are you?"

"You make it sound like an accusation."

"I don't mean to pry," Justina said stiffly.

"Oh, Jussie, you're not prying. You're my sister. All right. Yes, life is treating me well. Sure, I'm happy. The quartet is doing well. I'm meeting new people. I've got a few good friends. Things are all right."

"I'm worried to death about LeeLee." Justina rushed on. "She's with a group of girls who love her one day and dump her the next. I never know when I pick her up after school if she's going to come out laughing about some secret they've shared or crying because they told her all the seats in study hall were taken and she'd have to sit somewhere else."

Mae, who was used to the way her sister's mind worked, leapt easily with her into this new topic. "It sounds like she needs to find some new friends."

"That's what I keep telling her. What kind of friends keep you hanging up in the air like that, I ask her. Why do you want to wait around for someone to decide whether or not they'll take you in? You ought to have more self-respect. So I'm the one that gets screamed at: I'm the one who doesn't understand, who's pushing her around where I want her to be."

"What a mess," Mae said. "But girls are like that, aren't they? I mean, they all seem to go through a stage of being catty and hateful to each other."

"We didn't."

"No? Well, you wouldn't remember. You would have been the one in charge of things. You always were the popular one."

"Was I?" Justina asked, the wistfulness in her voice begging so evidently for reassurance that there had been a time when she had a personality which other people took notice of, that Mae gave in and said it again, conscious that they had, once again, shifted from discussing Justina's children to discussing Justina.

"You were the popular one," she repeated more firmly, trying to conjure up for her sister the reality of those days when she was Jussie Cavin and all the world knew it. Even as she repeated it, she saw them, the two Cavin sisters, hurrying up the sidewalk to town before the stores closed. Justina naturally took the inside of the walk; Mae strode dutifully beside and a bit behind. Justina's white socks clung to her ankles in trim white folds, her loafers patted through the leaves. Mae's feet slapped down at every step; when she looked down at her shoes, they seemed to stretch far out before her like rust-colored flippers.

"It's almost six," Justina warned. "Mr. Hanks'll close." They had to buy two cartons of whipping cream because Mama's Winchester cousins had called while they were in the middle of fixing supper to announce that they wanted to drive over tomorrow afternoon and show off the new baby. Mama had been caught out without a thing in the world to serve them except some peach preserves left from summer. Sugar was so short. "An upside-down cake will do," she decided, snapping her apron over the porch rail to free it of bean strings. "Girls, you run up to the store and get me some whipping cream."

"Money, Mama," Mae had to remind her, waiting unhappily at the screen door as her mother came inside. Justina was already at the hall mirror, fixing her hair.

"Yes." Mama sighed, looking briefly at her scuffed black patent leather handbag on the mantelpiece. "You'll have to raid the teapot, I guess." Mae lifted the chipped china pot from its corner shelf and dug through scraps of paper and old stamps and unmatched buttons to the pennies at the bottom. Once the pot had held all kinds of change, filled to the brim with nickels and dimes and even a few quarters which Papa emptied from his pockets when he came in at night. The pennies made Mae's hand smell of dirty metal. Mama gave her a handkerchief to carry them in.

"You'd think we'd never *seen* a new baby before," Justina said as they left Mama to finish setting out supper. She kept fingering her hair where it lay against her shoulders. "Does it look all right? Is the curl right?" though she had posed in front of the mirror not five minutes before. At fourteen, Mae had already learned that much of her sister's talk was a kind of background noise; Justina paid less attention to what she said than to how she looked, and probably assumed that everyone else did, too. So Mae didn't bother to answer. Of course Justina looked lovely and of course she knew it and anyone could see that it was her younger sister who was hopeless (even now walking to town in overalls), whose lank colorless hair was so impossible that Mama said it was a waste of precious money to have it worked on at Miss Rose's Beauty Salon and cut it at home herself.

"You're about the slowest person I ever walked with," Justina said, but absently, her attention on the boys in the front seat of a passing Chevy. Mae followed along behind, struck into silence by her sister's radiant confidence, now that there were people around. Justina looked them straight in the eye and spoke to each one of them and then smiled. Mae watched her feet slap down on the sidewalk, keeping track of how many leaves her shoe crushed with one blow. The pennies were warm and heavy in her hand. Her feet slowed when Justina's did, shuffled uneasily in the leaves while her sister talked to some high school boys. The sidewalk had crumbled to nothing in front of the filling station. Mae looked up in time to recognize that it was Robert Combs on the corner reading the new movie poster; Justina had slowed down again and was smoothing out her full skirt. Would he ask her now? Mae wondered. There he was reading all about the movie and here was Justina prettier than ever. It was Robert Combs' eyelashes that Justina talked about at night while she brushed her hair and Mae waited for her to turn the light out. Justina said they were just dreamy. Surely he would ask her now. Mama would let her go with him. The movie would be over by nine and it was barely a ten-minute walk home. Of course, Robert Combs' father was the town lawyer and Daddy didn't believe in lawyers, but he hadn't said anything when Robert stopped to talk to Justina that time after church. Robert Combs always wore deep-colored sweaters which made his shoulders look even broader than they were. This afternoon it was a burgundy sweater, Mae noted with satisfaction. He must have seen them, for he turned away from the poster and was just standing there, like he was waiting for them. He would certainly ask her now. Robert Combs smiled, and Mae's fingers uncurled and dropped pennies all over the sidewalk. Heads spinning, pennies ran across the road, down the hill, spilled into the gutter.

"Oh, for pity's sake," Justina said.

There goes Mama's whipping cream, Mae thought. She watched pennies roll and bury themselves beneath a year's worth of leaves. Pinching Mama's handkerchief between thumb and forefinger, she waved it gently in the air. One last coin dropped out.

Robert Combs walked over to them, grinning. Justina smiled prettily back and shrugged her shoulders slightly to disclaim all responsibility for her little sister.

"I guess we'd better help your sister catch her change or she'll miss getting her ice cream cone tonight." He sprinted beautifully into the street, scooping up pennies as he ran. Justina knelt and retrieved several that had fallen beside her toe. Mae scooped handfuls of wet leaves from the gutter, sifting through them for metal. Her fingernails grew black with mud. Robert Combs panted up beside her. "Here," he said. He cupped her hands and poured a pile of pennies in, careful as Mama measuring sugar from the sack. "Hang onto that now," he told her, not unkindly. "You might want to count it. I don't know how many we lost. You might not have enough for that ice cream." His hands, as he folded hers into place around the coins, were dry and rough. Why, Mae wondered, hadn't she worn something besides her brother's old shirt with these overalls. She was too embarrassed by the touch of Robert Combs' hands to explain to him what the money was for. He had probably seen her often enough eating ice cream with Pike Lenox, Pike's mouth ringed with chocolate.

Justina moved beside them, her skirt swaying just a little. "Are you ready now?" she asked her sister. Just then Robert Combs put his hand on her arm. "You're coming to see the movie with me Saturday, aren't you?" Justina looked up at him. "Maybe," she said. Then, "All right," but slowly, not teasing him, exactly, but not letting him know either that he was the one she talked to Mae about at night. "Take care of the kid," he called after them.

When they got to Mr. Hanks' store, Justina was just as anxious as Mae to dump the money out on the counter and count it to see if they had enough. It wasn't, Mae thought, watching the two of them walk back down the hill, the sack tucked firmly under the arm of the sister who lumbered after the slighter figure in front swaying, graceful as a dancer in her full skirt, it wasn't that Justina was selfish. She just had a natural flair for turning any situation to her own advantage.

"Do you remember Robert Combs?" she asked her sister suddenly.

"Who?"

After all, Justina had only gone out with him that one time. "He's a bit short," she had commented, brushing out her hair after the movie. Mae sat in bed waiting to hear every detail. But Justina said there wasn't much to tell. Robert Combs kept calling, but Justina refused to talk to him, and Mae had had to listen to him, his voice husky and hesitant with embarrassment, ask if she knew what he had done wrong. "It's nothing you did," she finally told him. "It's just Justina." Which was as close as she could come then to articulating the way her older sister used people when she needed them, left them behind when her eyes seized on finer sights. Managing people had been her main gift, and that she could no longer exercise it must be a source of continual frustration. But she had no one with whom she could get away with that anymore.

"Robert Combs?" Justina's voice interrupted her thoughts. "Was he an old boyfriend of yours?"

"No," Mae told her. "Yours. You were the popular one."

"Was I really?" Justina sounded as delighted as a child. "Oh, you're just saying that. But what I really want to know is, will you come for Thanksgiving? It's going to be a real family time, and if you were here it would be just perfect."

"So, you had this terrible dream," Andy prompted. He had invited himself along to listen to the dress rehearsal, and, now that it was over, was lounging in Mae's chair, feet propped on the rung of the chair in front. The stage had cleared quickly, the musicians eager to get home after a long evening. At his podium, Jason Dewar talked quietly with the section leaders. The orchestra manager, a thick-set woman in a purple sweater, bustled from stand to stand collecting music.

Mae wiped a last smear of rosin from her violin before laying it in its case. "You know how you can be so caught in a dream that you feel as though it's happening to you right then and there, and it hangs over you even after you've gotten up? I had to turn on the lights and walk around for awhile."

The stage lights dimmed, with a dramatic pause between each darkening as though whoever controlled the switch was exulting in a new-found power. A final row of lights was snapped off with a heavy click: center stage went black.

"We're not through out here," Jason Dewar called impatiently. He glared backstage, his hand frozen in mid-gesture, until the circle of light swelled around him again. Dust motes danced down the brilliant shaft to the white square of his music.

"What did you dream about?" Andy asked, pressing her as though it were the most natural thing in the world that he should be privy to her dreams. In the last weeks, he had acted as though he had noticed no change in her treatment of him, demanding, by his persistent normal friendliness, that she trust him as she always had, until she began to believe that she had never formed misapprehensions about their relationship, nor been startled into doubting them. Andy was simply an old, dear friend with whom she had never gotten serious. Even as she spoke, all feeling of estrangement faded, and she confided herself to the grey eyes which regarded her as steadily as they ever had.

"Well, it wasn't all a dream. That is, it wasn't all my dream." Her voice trailed off.

"You're right, that sounds ridiculous," Andy beat his feet against the metal chair rung. "So tell me already."

"I dreamt that I was lying in bed listening to someone cry. Crying and crying, somewhere in another room, and no one went to see what was wrong."

"You probably heard that kid downstairs from you. Remember the time we heard him screaming and you ran down in your bathrobe to find out what was wrong and it turned out his parents had left him alone for a few minutes while they went to the corner to buy cigarettes?"

"We're through here now," Jason Dewar called to someone hovering in the wings. "Shut 'em off." The section leaders moved ponderously offstage, heads bent. It had not been an entirely satisfactory last rehearsal, and Mae wondered if Andy's interest in her dream was one way he could delay giving his opinion of the orchestra. The lights went out, this time with only a flicker of time between each one. In the darkness, smells suddenly sprang alive; the sharp scent of Andy's aftershave burst through the gloom like a lemon squeezed. Behind them, the heavy curtains hanging in thick folds exuded the dust of forgotten concerts. As someone moved backstage, the floorboards thumped, then came a silence as deep as if a stone were rolled into place at the entrance to a tomb, though, Mae reminded herself, they had only to push open the backstage door and the rattle of traffic would quickly link them to the living city. Meanwhile, shut into this place which was built for public revelation, Mae felt she could tell Andy anything, even confess her increasing attraction to Jason Dewar.

Andy's voice roused her. "You'd make a lousy storyteller. Your audience would be asleep before you got through your introduction."

"Which is perhaps why she's a musician instead." Jason Dewar stood beside her, his arms empty, for once, of music. In the dark his eyes glinted as he looked first at her, then at Andy. "I hope I'm not interrupting anything." He added, more stiffly. "They're closing up and you're likely to get locked inside. Which is not a pleasant prospect on a chilly fall night. Our stage manager appears to be one of the few people at this university who goes after her job with a vengeance. This place will be freezing in a few minutes."

"We were just leaving," Mae said.

"Not me." Andy shoved his hands in his pockets and slouched still lower in his chair. "I'm waiting for my story." He looked up at Jason Dewar. "Mae was telling me about a nightmare she had last night."

"And I thought I was the one in this orchestra with the nightmares."

"Good lord, Andy, you make it sound so important. I simply had a dream about someone crying. Nothing dramatic, nothing psychic, and certainly nothing to keep us standing around here any longer. Especially since Mr. Dewar has the concert to get through tomorrow."

"Of course. Good night, you two." Turning on his heel, Jason Dewar strode offstage, choosing, Mae noted, the path between the first and second violinists' chairs by which every conductor departs the concert stage.

"No love lost between the two of you, is there?" Andy unfolded himself from his chair.

But the dream had been important to her, and walking silently beside Andy on the way home, she tried to think it straight in her mind. She had dreamed of someone crying, then must have awakened just enough to realize she was dreaming, to recall, with a swoop into the past, what the dream reminded her of. She was staying with Justina and Daniel. One night, she woke to hear Danny crying in his room. She listened for a few minutes, waiting for one of his parents to wake and go to him, then got out of bed and hurried down the hall to his room. A very young Danny leaned against the pillows of a bed several years too long for him. His face was damp with tears and sweat, feverish from crying. Mae pulled his teddy bear from the tangle of blankets at his feet, then smoothed the covers over him. It's all right, she murmured over and over. It's all right. She stroked the dark wet tendrils of hair which clung to his head. It's all right; it was just a dream. When his face began to relax, his eyes to focus on her, and he seemed to be listening to her voice, she asked quietly, do you want to tell me about it?

He choked on a final sob and hugged his bear. There was a witch. At the end of my bed. His voice wobbled. She was a big witch, with skinny hands. She had a black dress on and a tall black hat and her hair stuck out from under it like spikes. She was stirring a big pot that had lots of smoke coming out of it. Then she caught me looking at her and her eyes got really mean and she was going to cook me.

Mae pulled him close, resting her chin on top of his head. She rocked him, crooning, it's all right, Danny, it's all right. She rubbed his back with slow large circles. When his breathing slowed, she laid him back on his pillows. There now, see? There's no one at the foot of your bed. There's no one in your room but you and me. Nothing else, Danny. Witches are just in fairy tales. You remember how they always begin. Once-upon-a-time. That means a long, long time ago. There aren't any witches now.

Gradually, his eyes darkened, became blank, his eyelids dropped and closed, then fluttered open. I'll stay here until you're sound asleep, Mae promised. His eyes flickered in response, and he was asleep. She sat beside him for a few more minutes, her hand resting on his stomach. Very gently she lifted her hand, watching his face for any sign of wakefulness. He flung one arm back over his head, but didn't open his eyes. Gingerly, so the mattress wouldn't creak, she got up from the bed. Before turning down the light, she checked that the humidifier had enough water. It gurgled and steamed busily below his bed; with a start, she recognized his witch's kettle. Then it was that her own dreaming took over again, and in her dream, she didn't leave the room, didn't set the door open so that she would hear Danny if he awoke again. In her dream, she was still sitting with Danny on his bed, holding him while he cried and choked out his nightmare. As he talked, she looked to where he pointed at the end of his bed and there a tall figure in black hunched over the steam. It raised its head slowly to stare back at her, and then Mae hugged Danny tightly to her, for this was no fairy tale witch face of warty nose and spoky hair, but the beautiful, bemused face of her sister Justina.

Applause for the Brahms was enthusiastic and long. Jason Dewar passed Mae's chair twice to return to center stage, where he bowed and took the concertmaster's hand, then raised his orchestra, with a final grand upward sweep of both arms, to acknowledge the audience. "Bravo," he mouthed silently as he walked off for the last time. A slight smile pulled at the corner of his mouth.

Mae stood with the others until it was clear that he wasn't coming back. The applause died to a scattered clapping from those waiting, coats and hats on, to battle the crowds in the aisles. The concertmaster sat to let the orchestra sit, then twisted around to congratulate his section. All discipline broke: the prim black and black-and-white torsos sagged against chair backs, bent double to beat on friends' shoulders, twisted to call congratulations. When the concertmaster finally rose to leave, the others buzzed off in every direction, some pushing towards the side stairs to join friends in the audience, some rushing to the opposite side of the stage to exchange hugs. The harsh footlights were shut off, and Mae could see without squinting the crowd still slowly pushing its way to the exits, the stream blocked, trickling one body at a time around a beaming woman who had stopped to wave her program at one of the musicians.

"It wasn't so bad," Mae said to a flutist who waited beside her to get off stage.

"Are you kidding? They wouldn't have recognized us as the same orchestra if we weren't playing in the university auditorium.

We've never gotten a standing ovation before."

The keyed-up chatter of those already packing up bounced and re-echoed from the high ceiling of the rehearsal room. The noise was a physical presence, clapping Mae on the back, catching her by both arms. It was more overwhelming than sitting in the middle of the great final vibrating chords of Brahms. Mae spotted her things on a far table, half-covered by a heap of coats, and pushed towards them when the noise dropped away. Hands lifted cigarettes to lips which stilled before they were reached; the hands suspended, manikin-style, in mid-air; laughter froze to open-mouthed smiles. Mae alone continued moving as the orchestra manager swept to the center of the room with a swirl of black velvet.

"We'll meet at Dr. Finney's in 45 minutes." The firm, deep voice allowed no excuses. "That gives you plenty of time to get your instruments packed up. Don't go home and change, and don't stop off anywhere along the way. Come exactly as you are. Dr. Finney will want to see you all." Gesturing to one of the lesser officers to follow, she moved through the still-silent crowd, without, Mae realized, giving a word about their performance.

"So Dr. Finney didn't come?" she asked the flutist, who stood beside her buttoning a long coat.

"Of course not. He trusts us to do a good job," and she was gone, clutching her little case. More somberly now, the musicians gathered their things and left, those fresh from the stage quickly falling in with the mood of those who were leaving. The triumph of the evening, their mastery of the Brahms and Jason Dewar's brief smile of recognition, this was gone, and in their restrained expressions, their careful lack of enthusiasm, Mae could see them reclaiming their former arrogance. The concert was over; why all the excitement? Of course they had done a good job, why shouldn't they have? They were musicians, and good ones. Dr. Finney always said so.

If she had asked, at that moment, who their conductor was, she didn't doubt that the reply would have been Junius Finney, and that only if she pressed would anyone have added, oh yes, well for tonight this man, Jason Dewar, conducted. And did a pretty fair job of it.

Mae slipped out the side door and breathed deeply of the clean fall air. In the squares of light from the auditorium windows, the top of each tree sprang into life, each yellowed leaf given a stark outline against the black sky. She moved around the corner, head tipped back, her face tingling as if fresh-scrubbed in the chill night. In a wide window over the main stairwell, heads bobbed into sight. A slight woman plainly dressed carried a sleeping child. Behind her a small boy's legs pumped down the stairs and then his square face appeared at the landing window and then the back of his blonde head as he raced on down. Probably the bassoonist's family, Mae decided, hurrying to find their daddy and get their post-concert ice cream. She tasted her own post-concert ritual: a deep hot bath with a glass of sherry on the floor within easy reach, clean towels warmed over the heater, bed, with a new book bought that morning.

Around the next corner, down one flight of stairs, their shoulders not much above her own, the remaining musicians milled about the rehearsal room. The men were sleek in their black; about the women was more of uniform, less of elegance: no flashing rings or necklaces, no bare arms or shoulders, nothing which might distract and hold the listener's eye to individual beauty. Below these windows a double door opened wide to admit a platform that angled down to the orchestra van. The bass players and percussionists, coats off, sleeves rolled back, loaded their instruments. Shouts echoed from the metal cave of the van.

"I think we'd better dunk Jim in Finney's pool for missing that entrance in the third movement."

Something heavy was dragged across the van floor with a screech of metal. "Don't bother; we'll just let Jason Dewar take care of him."

A young brass player leaned out of the window, caution in his face. "You guys don't want to be late for the party."

Mae skirted the van, staying in its shadow, then stepped back onto the sidewalk, passing quickly beneath a last window where a couple embraced, hidden from their colleagues by a discarded choral riser. Trailing her hand along the rough brick, Mae turned the last corner of the building, back where she'd begun. She glanced automatically at the square of light above. A single bare light bulb hung from the middle of the ceiling, forbidding any trace of shadow in the tiny box of a room. Jason Dewar stood, half-turned towards the window. The harsh light allowed no softening of the planes of his face. His eyes were tired, somewhat abstracted as he studied a cigarette held between thumb and forefinger, stretching his arm away from him as if relaxing a cramped muscle. As he drew his arm back, he looked down at Mae. At first, he didn't recognize her. Hers was simply one more pale face in the darkness upturned to stare at him, though some trick of stage lighting left her features clear, and he stared back at her coolly, still listening to the phrase which had blurred in the last movement. Then the cigarette touched his lips, and as he breathed in, he recognized that he was not on stage but in the closet-sized cubicle arranged for him by the music department after he had raised a fuss. The woman didn't go away. He exhaled, daring her to keep spying on him. Then his eyes narrowed and he watched her with the pulsing alertness they had shared in rehearsal. It lasted a minute only, while Mae's insides knotted and churned, and then she forced herself to walk as naturally as she could manage around the building out of his sight.

There she hesitated. The last of the audience straggled down the steps. Mae shut her eyes and wrapped her arms tightly around her waist. I'm not going to do this, she told herself. I'm not going to let this happen. But, slowing only to lift the front of her long black skirt so she wouldn't trip, she ran lightly up the steps and through the lobby, down the carpeted aisle to the deserted stage, and back to the almost empty rehearsal room. She caught up with Lem and his cellist friend as they opened the door, interrupting them with a breathless smile as though they had been friends all along. "Could you give me a ride out to Dr. Finney's? Would you mind? I don't have my car and I'd hate to miss our party."

Sometime after night had crossed over to morning, Mae found herself sitting on the edge of a swimming pool with her legs up to the knees in water. She was quite warm: the pool was inside a glassed-in patio at the back of the house and heated to a constant 82 degrees. It was just long enough for Dr. Finney to do his laps, thirty of them, in the morning before he took his orange juice and whole-wheat cereal. Mae had a dim remembrance of Mrs. Finney explaining this to her when they met at the front door, or, at any rate, soon after they had passed from the smiled acknowledgement that they "shared" a seat in the orchestra to a mutual, groping silence caused, Mae saw too late, by her referring to it as "Mr. Dewar's orchestra." Mrs. Finney sent her to the outdoor bar for her first drink, whispering that she really must go check up on her husband.

Because the water was so warm, warmer even than the sticky air of the patio, it had taken Mae a long time to become aware of the fact that she was wet up to her knees. She had no idea where her shoes could be. She was grateful that she'd had the presence of mind to draw up her long dress so that only one edge of the hem had gotten damp. Other guests had not shared her prescience; several women near the door stood as if naked, their figures outlined by the wet cloth clinging to them. A very young cellist who had, Mae believed, shared the back seat with Lem's friend on the drive over, was perched on the diving board wearing only a wide towel. Her wet hair had been twisted up and pinned in the back and someone had thrust a chopstick or shishkabob skewer through it, geisha-girl style. Mae didn't see how she could have done that by herself.

Mae shifted her hand on the scratchy indoor-outdoor carpet and struck a squat glass of melting ice cubes. She picked it up and drank until the cubes rattled, then set the glass down too close to the pool's edge. It tipped into the water, bobbing up and down in the false cheerful blue. When she bent to scoop it out, she was captivated by the sight of her legs, which stretched on forever, thin and wavering, the lights in the pool wall giving them a ghostly white glow.

There were also lights strung through the trees that grew in formal intervals between the indoor and outdoor patios, and, less restrained, in a grove at the far end of the yard. These crowded together and suggested that the garden was enclosed by a deep and shadowed forest. The tree lights were too bright to look at directly, though they were nothing more than strings of the tiny white fairy lights that are draped around Christmas trees. These pinpoints of brilliance did little to illuminate the gravel paths which wound through the grove, and Mae saw the dark shapes of couples edging away from the crowd into the shadows. Others had retreated to the house to collapse on Mrs. Finney's lavender-and-cream-covered armchairs. The small space around the outdoor bar was crowded with dancers, the younger musicians, who had pushed back the glass tables and claimed their territory. Every now and then the crowd would split open and one figure would emerge and dance away, jerking, spinning, snapping fingers, while those watching clapped him on and cheered. One danced through the doorway of the inner patio, still spinning, gesturing to his audience, coming closer and closer to the diving board where the towel-clad girl leaned on one elbow, watching. With a final twirl, though at no particular climax in the music that Mae could discern, he leapt into the pool. She drew back, less bothered by the splash than by the yells of those who came running to pull the dancer out.

The noise startled her, and for a moment she was at school again, a clumsy 15-year-old clinging to the side of the gymnasium's pool while their swimming teacher blasted a whistle and yelled for Mae to let go of the wall. Half of the class swam with desperate splashing strokes down to the shallow end; the other girls sat shivering on the wet tile bench built into the wall, jeering at those in the pool. There was a continual roar, as if they were beside the sea, caused by water rushing against the pool's sides and the girls' screams bouncing against the tile walls and ceiling. Mae let go at last, afraid the teacher would pry her fingers from the pool side, and cast herself, flailing, gasping, fighting the water which burned her nose and seemed to fight back at her as she swam after the other girls.

The dancer shook his wet clothes vigorously, and his friends drew back, screeching. They caught his arms before he could spray them again, and dragged him into the house to change.

"Did he get you wet?" A young man hung by his arms from the diving board, grinning at the girl above. She simply shook her head and returned her attention to the center of the dance floor. She must be waiting for someone, too, thought Mae. And he hasn't noticed yet. Too bad; there was a charm in the elemental nature of her plans: she had removed her clothes, she had arranged her hair, she waited. How rude that he just ignored her, whoever he was. He ought to have the decency to know that he was wanted.

Mae stirred the water with her legs, stretching them so the calves lay just along the surface. She flexed and pointed her toes, admiring the line of her legs, then raised her eyes to see, directly across the pool on the other side of the glass wall, Jason Dewar.

He held a cigarette in one hand, an empty glass in the other, listening to three women who stood so close that the one speaking could touch his arm for emphasis. Mae saw at once that they weren't musicians, as someone else might think 'they aren't Union,' and with as much disdain. They wore colors. The woman with her back to Mae, whose hand rested on Jason Dewar's arm, wore a green dress of a shiny fabric which glinted at each curve of waist and hip. Heavy gold bracelets slid up her arm as she raised a glass; the nails of the thin fierce hand gripping it were long and beautifully shaped. Mae thought of the time it must take to polish them, as well as the effort to maintain those bare shoulders, delicately molded with muscle. Jason said something in reply and the earrings of all three sparked as they nodded.

It was the earrings that did it. "I love you, but I'm not in love with you anymore." That had been the sentence that nearly ruined her last year at the conservatory, spoken by a young cellist whose career she had, in her imagination, entwined with her own for years to come. Spoken to her over a lovely dinner at an Italian restaurant while the woman in the booth behind him turned her head this way and that and laughed, long gold earrings sparkling in the candlelight. Mae had stared at the dance of those earrings while she tried to think of something to say. She hadn't been able to say anything, and so they had ended it. He had ended it. But now she would have the sense to argue back. What do you mean? she would demand. That sounds like an arbitrary distinction to me. Are you looking for an excuse to get out of the relationship, or what? Now, she would be able to make him admit his true motivations for dumping her, would woo him back if she wanted, but at least, above all, would not let him slip away from her with any complacency that he had gotten out gracefully, gotten out easily. Oh, she was wiser now. She trusted in her feelings and wouldn't any longer sit back passively and wait.

The woman in green spoke again, for her hand moved on Jason's arm and the eyes of the two shorter women darted back and forth. With no very clear purpose in mind, Mae pushed herself up from the pool with the vigor of a professional diver emerging after a successful dive, and strode through the patio door, shaking out her black skirt as she walked. She paused at the bar to refresh her drink, then made her way to the edge of a group just behind his left shoulder, close enough to brush casually against the nubbly texture of his black coat. She had to suppress an urge to dust off the cigarette ash sprinkled across his sleeve; the three women were already alert to her presence although, in unspoken communion, they pretended not to have noticed her. Even with her eyes on Dr. Finney's terrazzo floor, Mae was overwhelmed by him. His back seemed to grow straight from the ground. If she had dared, she could trace its perfect line with her finger. The black curve from shoulder to shoulder was so pure and distinct it nearly crackled, and the sudden stiff white of his shirt cuff made her want to curl back into the crowd. He was so real, so real and completely separate from her. In her imaginings of him, he had no substance, his voice or figure or presence appeared and disappeared at her desire. She had never dreamed of confronting him.

The voice of the woman in green was low, lush, confident of its audience. "And then, Jason, you simply must see how you like the Christmas celebration at the Blakely Manor. It is just the thing to put you in the mood for the season. Candles everywhere, and in the parlor a new choir every night." She settled her bracelets back in place.

"He'll surely need to wait and see just how busy he's going to be with the Messiah performances and all the concerts for the schoolchildren." The shortest woman spoke kindly.

"I'm sure that—" Jason began.

"Oh, lovely." The green dress shimmered in delight.

The third woman echoed her. "Yes, lovely. I just knew he would want to be counted in once he heard what a special place Blakely Manor is. Really, it raises more money than anything else the Symphony Guild does. And it is without any doubt the high point of our entire year."

"Not counting the concerts," the short woman added quickly.

"Exactly." The woman in green placed an arm briefly around her friend, though whether to draw her closer into the conversation or to hold her in her place, Mae wasn't sure. "Wasn't it a lovely performance? I know we all think so, Jason."

It was now or retreat to the pool to keep vigil with the girl in the towel. "Mr. Dewar," Mae said firmly. She planted her arm on that elegant black sleeve and steered him slightly away from the other three. "You promised several hours ago that you would speak with me. It's getting quite late. And it is imperative," she enunciated so clearly that her front teeth bit her lower lip, "that I speak with you tonight."

Having pointedly examined her rumpled black dress, the woman in green was staring at her feet. What had she done with her shoes? Mae wondered, then took another deep breath and smiled at the three. "Orchestra business, you know. Do you mind?" This last was addressed to the women, though it was Jason to whom she looked, sliding her hand into the crook of his elbow and leaning against him with an air of comradely assertiveness.

"If you'll excuse me." He gave the women a slight bow, implying rather than promising that he would return.

"You need another drink," Mae told him when she had moved him safely away. "When you're at a party, you shouldn't stand for so long with an empty glass or the same woman. It's not partylike."

"I hadn't realized it had been such a long time. Since I finished my drink, I mean." He was possibly as drunk as she was.

"Well," Mae said, "the bar's this way."

The bartender, hired till two, had gone home. Lem stood behind the bar, pouring beer into a carefully-angled glass. The girl in the towel, a man's overcoat belted around her now, was perched on a cooler beside him.

"Two bourbons, please." Mae folded her arms on the counter and leaned closer to watch Lem fill their glasses. "You make a better bartender than you do a musician, don't you think? Have you ever thought of changing careers?"

"Only if I keep meeting beautiful women." He wrapped his free arm around the girl, who smiled vaguely. She clutched her towel in two fists as a child does its favorite blanket.

Mae took the glasses. "Thanks. I appreciate it. Mr. Dewar appreciates it. We all appreciate it."

"Mr. Dewar?" the girl repeated, sitting up straight.

"Cheers." Mae handed him a glass. "Drink up. However long our night was, I expect yours has been even longer."

"Shall we?" He lowered himself carefully onto a bench built around a poplar. Mae sat beside him. "It wasn't as bad as it might have been," he said after a judicious sip. "In places, they sounded quite powerful."

"*We* sounded, you mean."

"So, you consider yourself a member of the orchestra now." It was half-question, half-banter.

"It's gotten to be almost a habit." Mae smiled. "Like flossing your teeth. You know, you do it because you know it's good for you. After awhile you don't notice anymore how much time it takes."

"My father would have been delighted by the comparison." Jason Dewar finished off his drink. "He wanted me to be a dentist. 'Now, that's a reliable profession,' he used to say. 'You're always needed.'"

Mae leaned towards him, her chin resting on her elbow which rested on her knee. She swung her crossed leg back and forth, perilously close to Jason Dewar's elegant black trousers. "Well," she demanded, "what about you? Do you feel part of the orchestra?"

He actually smiled. "You mean as much as a conductor can feel a part of the orchestra. You all do get to sit down, remember." He gazed at the empty glass he turned between his fingers. "Don't psychologists claim that working together towards a common goal forges bonds between even the most dissimilar types?"

She couldn't resist. "Especially when such a fine example of trust and concern is modelled for us by our fearless leader."

"Well, you choose," and his voice snapped at her. "Music, or a mutual admiration society, a what-do-they-call-it, a support group. Where everybody's accepted for what they are. No matter what they could be if they were tough enough or far-sighted enough or smart enough to tolerate a little embarrassment and discipline for the sake of something beyond the sacred self and its beloved insecurities."

"Are you speaking of me, Mr. Dewar?" Mae sat up, away from him, planting both feet squarely on the ground.

He slumped a little, as if some part of him were caving in on itself, and in silence they watched the dancers repeating the same step over and over to a long percussive interlude on the tape. Mae wondered how much it bothered him, his isolation from those he had devoted his last months to. Even this party was more a reunion for Dr. Finney and his orchestra than a celebration of their successful performance with Jason Dewar.

"No," he said finally, "of course I wasn't speaking about you."

The tape ended, and the musicians across the patio clapped, couples mixing with other couples in sudden conversation. Mae asked, "What's wrong with a compromise?"

He turned to her. The fairy lights that twinkled above them cast dappled shadows across his face, giving it a restless and strangely uncertain look. "Would you really like it if I conducted according to what they want, or think they want?" He frowned at the squeals of laughter coming from the pool. "Soon enough there wouldn't be any music worth listening to, just noise from those unwilling to make up their minds what it is they want, or unwilling to work to get it." He dismissed the dancers with a flick of his wrist and Mae had to smile. He was so impatient with them, yet so right. The music crooning across to them now was sweet unto sickness, its rhythms predictable, its words saying whatever fit the rhyme scheme. Swaying intently to the melody, the musicians bent serious faces to their partners. Mae spotted Lem, clutching a plump second violinist, the little cello player nowhere in sight.

"You've been good for them." Having offered him that much, she had to continue. "I've enjoyed playing under you. There's a kind of richness in orchestral playing which I wouldn't have believed before. It was only last year that Andy had to twist my arm before I'd go to a symphony concert."

"So you dragged me over here to thank me for providing you with quality entertainment?" he asked dryly.

Mae stood. "I didn't, as you say, drag you over here to tell you anything, Mr. Dewar. I offered you a chance to escape from the Symphony Guild Society ladies, to whom you are more than welcome to return."

"I'm sorry." The weight of his hand on her arm forced her to sit. "Perhaps I have seemed overbearing with the group, perhaps I've been too strict. But let me tell you why." He waited for her nod before continuing. "When I came here in August, the orchestra was flailing around with no sense of unity, no understanding of the power there is in being one body of musicians. Don't misunderstand me. There are some fine individual players. Dr. Finney was a great clarinetist in his time, and attracted many talented instrumentalists to the department." Mae just caught herself from smiling; even in giving his predecessor the praise without which no self-justification rings true, Jason Dewar was careful to stick to fact: Dr. Finney was, once, a great clarinetist.

"But they had no sense of group discipline, and no idea of how they must, as musicians, bond together to form an orchestra."

"A great concert soloist doesn't necessarily make a good quartet member." Mae dreamily repeated the rule, some fragment of practice room wisdom from years ago. For the first time it sounded to her like a positive statement, yielding room in the scheme of things for all levels of talent, rather than the sour-grapes excuse of a fellow student sniffing, after a crushing audition. "Well, I can always get a job in some quartet."

Jason ignored her interjection. "They were too accustomed to enjoying themselves and their rapport with Dr. Finney to discover how hard they could push themselves."

"They were lazy," Mae supplied.

"I think so." He set his glass on the ground with the decisive air of one who has concluded an argument, leaving no room for doubt or questions. Mae felt irritation rise in her again.

"And under you they have shown their potential as a professional orchestra, and until tonight's party, no one could stand to be around anyone else."

"If you like."

"Hasn't it crossed your mind that just occasionally it might be good for them to feel that you valued them as human beings and not merely as music makers?"

He looked at her as he had when they first met, as though again summing her up and finding her wanting. "My job is to care about the way they sound, Miss Cavin. It no more matters to me what they are like as individuals than it matters what kind of clothes the audience is wearing. The point is, how does the musician play, how hard is he willing to work, can he—does he—bring the music to life."

He pushed on and his face changed again, the lines about the mouth softening, so that Mae felt another pang as she realized he'd forgotten her completely. "Music is so different from the other arts. For musicians, I mean; I'm not talking about composers. For us, the music exists long before we come to it. It is there on the page, in black notes you must read."

She had to interrupt him, to remind him she was there. "So we're readers, then, that's all."

"Let me finish. It exists here, also, in the air, an ideal melody and tone waiting on us to translate it into actual sound which anyone may share. We're not just readers, nothing so passive. We're translators for those who want to hear but who aren't able to until it is made accessible to them. And some of us, we have the gift of hearing while the music is only an ideal." He sighed. "How can we refuse to follow that command? How can we not at least try to translate faithfully? Knowing that of course we'll fail, that we can never hope to recreate the perfection that was in the composer's mind."

They watched the slow drift towards the house of departing guests. The tape player had long since shut down. Mrs. Finney flitted from group to group saying her good nights. As she approached their bench, Jason Dewar stood.

"Oh, please, stay, be comfortable, enjoy yourselves. We're off to bed, but that needn't mean you have to leave. I want Dr. Finney to get some rest. If you see him, would you please send him up to me?"

She started to scuttle away, then paused as if sensing something more should be said. "Thank you so much for coming. We heard that the concert was just lovely. Everyone enjoyed your playing. Good night, now."

"She doesn't know who you are," Mae whispered, glad of an excuse to say something and relieve the ache in her throat which was held-back tears, for he had forgotten all about her.

"Is it any wonder the man never took command of the orchestra," Jason Dewar whispered back. "He can't even choose his own bedtime."

This quiet sharing of laughter over something which, really, had no humor, made it all the harder. Mae felt it slipping from her, that

bright anticipation which had begun to glow inside when she pow-
dered her legs and arms with a new talc and, in her long silk slip
and black heels, tidied her apartment, waiting for the last minute
to finish dressing so her concert black wouldn't wrinkle. She had
sensed that something would happen tonight, something between
them would be resolved. The sweet golden sherry she alternately
sniffed and sipped had simply heightened her anticipation. It was
tonight that she would know whether those quick intent glances
exchanged during rehearsal were real or merely, once again, her
imagination. Even as she tasted the last drop of the sherry she
had shuddered; probably she'd made the whole thing up, just as
she was creating for herself the exultant mood which would make
exciting the concert.

It was fading now, that anticipation, and fading also, as she sat
beside the man, just as she had imagined, was the drunken thrill
of confidence with which she had walked away from those three
women, Jason Dewar following. Her hand ached to lie again on
the arm which lay inches from her on the bench. She should have
walked away from him when she'd stood behind him on the patio
and realized the power he had over her, walked away before she
revealed herself to him. Now anticipation rushed away like blood
from the head before a faint, and she ached with the dull certainty:
it can never happen, you dreamt it all, how silly of you, how embarrassing. Mae clutched his arm, almost crying out to hide her
shame: "But they are all so young, they are like children. They're
so fragile, so easily humiliated. You could break them to bits, no
matter how cynical, how tough they seem."

"You want me to baby them." The retort came so quickly that
she could only suppose he despised what she said. Or, and the
thought made her drop his arm as if it scorched her: perhaps he,
too, was desperate to keep the argument going if only because
it kept them face to face, kept them mauling one another, possibly tearing to the bone, but not indifferent, not politely, genteely,
cruelly, indifferent.

"Not baby them, exactly. But perhaps you could give them a
little more praise, or gentler criticism?" She wondered that he
didn't hear the plea beneath her words: notice *me*, praise *me*; then
hurried on, for he turned to her, interested in what she was say-

ing. She spoke thinking not particularly of Lem or his cellist friend or of the young men with precisely-clipped moustaches and tight sweaters who made up the percussion section or even of the aging but still proudly-rowdy brass players in their baseball caps, but of them all and of some generalized figure she called musician. "I don't think that musicians grow up very well. They don't really finish maturing the way most people do. Maybe because they spend so many hours of their adolescence alone, working for the most beautiful tone, the most perfectly modulated phrase, while normal kids are worrying over how their hair looks and who will call them that night. The musician gets so absorbed in working towards that ideal sound of yours that other things get neglected. So when they do run into those other things—oh, you know, money problems, illnesses, unexpected babies—they tend to fall apart. They never learned to think of things like that as other than trivial, as interruption, in comparison with their work. They aren't prepared for how disruptive those trivialities can become. All their lives they were trained to ignore those trivial details which to most people are lives."

"You are, perhaps, speaking of me, Miss Cavin?" His voice was ironic, yet he didn't seem angry at her, his arms spread behind them on the bench. She supposed that they were far now from the area in which she might wound him, force him into angry defense of his professional pride. As long as she talked of personalities, even, abstractly, of his own, without touching on his work, probably what she had to say wouldn't matter all that much.

"I don't know that I meant to." Desire to touch him muffled her tone. "Words are so imprecise, aren't they? I mean, I'm not always sure what it is I've just said. There are so many meanings behind a single word. You might hear something I've said in a completely different way than I meant it. You would never play for anyone like that, never perform a quartet unless you knew absolutely how each trill should come out. I don't know you well enough to know if you are one of those people who hides behind the ideal and ignores the trivial. Or if you are one of those for whom the existence of an ideal so intensifies the pain of the trivial that you are unable to ignore it. Though you claim to."

"I think you're still asking me to compromise." But there was a smile in his voice.

"Well, you must be aware of other people sometimes. I mean, you do have a family." She stopped. His wife was still, as gossip had it, in Cleveland, the boy, caught in between, away at school. There always seemed to be a child caught in between. Like Danny. She hadn't properly thought of Danny since she had become so absorbed in the orchestra. She really ought to find out what he intended to do about Thanksgiving. She would call him tomorrow.

"Surely you of all people" (why her of all people, she wondered; what did he know about her that he appeared not to know?) can see that if I disturb the balance of power between myself and the orchestra it will be the music which will suffer, which will be interrupted by our little emotions and relationships, by questions and worries and all the minor upsets that ought to be left offstage. All the petty things we come to music to forget."

"I thought music was born from understanding of just those petty things," Mae replied softly.

"So you're saying it's been a mistake that I lived my whole life believing that music is the most important thing there is, that my ability to hear it and pass it along so that others share what I hear was more important than anything else. You're saying that I've been living under a delusion; that I've been self-indulgent; that I've simply created a justification for exercising tyranny over other people. And that there's been something more important all along." He looked frantically around as though he might discover, on the back patio of Dr. Finney's house, just what that was. "Sunday dinner with the family, neighbors dropping in after church, everyone sitting in the living room without worrying about the dishes, no one saying much since they talked all through the meal. Too wet to go for a walk, so the men wait for the ball game to come on, and the women flip through magazines." He waved his hand, a feeble imitation of his usual commanding gesture. "My family never had a Sunday like that. I was out at a rehearsal, or I was in my study going over a score. Abby kept the house quiet so I could concentrate. If Tim turned on a ball game, I didn't hear it. If he went to one, it wasn't with me. Abby found plenty of other men to take her to my concerts." His laugh was more like a snort.

"They must have understood. It was your work." She had

wanted to reach him; she hadn't wanted to hurt him. Her voice sought excuses for him.

"My work. Music floating through my head cutting off the noise of the outside world. Abby used to say it just like that: 'your work,' in a kind of holy, reverent tone, and then flit out the back door the minute I'd gone back to my study."

"So what else would you have chosen?" She had to pull him back. "To be a dentist like your father wanted? Working nine-to-five with an hour off for lunch and a pretty hygienist to flirt with while you work on someone's mouth?"

He stared a long while at his hands. Long, muscular, they rested on his knees in unaccustomed stillness. No pulse of life in them now. They were hands any man might use to grip a shovel in the back garden or guide a lawn mower or, in search of youthful excitement as they grew past middle age, caress the wheel of a new sports car. Mae thought, watching him study his hands, that he must look as his father had on a rainy afternoon when he was unable to get outside to his toolshed and his lawn, surely a stern, hardworking man who took off his tie on Friday evening and looked forward to a weekend of chores.

"Nothing else, I suppose. I would have done the same. I had to." He glanced up at the lights which sparkled still, though the music had long since ended and car doors slammed in the drive.

"Then there's nothing to fret over, is there?" His wave of doubt had passed; she could feel him straighten up with the usual confidence. "Good thing," she said, making herself smile, clutching at last stores of energy so that they might pass lightly through this transition moment. "Where would the orchestra have been tonight without you?"

He accepted the shift into banter. "Home, I suppose, where they belonged."

"And where I ought to be right now." Mae stood, giddy from all that had happened. She wanted to dart away before they bogged down in the awkwardness of post-revelation. "I wonder where I left my shoes?" she murmured.

"Let me help you look for them." He loomed above her, his stiff, black coat almost brushing her shoulder.

"Oh, no, don't bother. I'm sure they must be in the house

somewhere. But thank you. Thank you for your company." She could tolerate no more; too many of her imaginings had been replaced by reality this evening. "Good night."

He followed her to the house, but there she stepped swiftly into the departing crowd and was hidden, lost to his sight as surely as if she'd run into the weaving shadows of the backyard trees. Jason Dewar looked once again out to the empty patio. On a webbed chair beside the pool a girl wept, her shoulders hunched forward as if to shield the head hanging between.

The morning after Dr. Finney's party, Mae woke up late, with a dull sense that something had happened that should not have happened. It took two cups of coffee carried back to bed before she knew that this reverse foreboding was due to no physical hangover. Yet her hands trembled so that the spoon clattered against the cup as she stirred her coffee. All her muscles were tensed against some impending onslaught of violence: noise, light, even the sudden shift of a pillow at her back. She looked apprehensively at the phone, expecting that at any minute it would ring and confirm her anticipation of disaster, its ring completing the jangling of her nerves. This shakiness, this sense of vulnerability, it was just what she remembered of mornings years ago when she had drunk too much and slept too little. But it wasn't that.

She hoped Andy wouldn't call. She wasn't ready to explain her sudden decision to go to a party she had sworn to him she would avoid. She couldn't lie about it; he would have called last night, he would know she hadn't come straight back from the concert. Neither could she tell him the truth: what was there to tell, anyway? She'd spent a few hours with a man she liked and then come home alone. It hadn't meant a thing. Jason Dewar had told her all sorts of things he probably regretted this morning. But that was the way with parties; people played confession as they'd once played spin the bottle. She wasn't silly enough to take the game seriously. Mae pushed her empty coffee cup onto the nightstand. Yet, there was something, something. We have done those things which we ought

not to have done. We have left undone those things which we
ought to have done. And there is no health in us. The old words
ran around her mind like doggerel.

At eleven, the phone rang.

"Mae, this is Jason Dewar."

"Yes," she said stupidly.

"I hope you got home all right. I would have driven you."

She ignored the faint reproof in his voice. "I was fine, really."

"I enjoyed talking with you last night," he said after a brief
pause. "I wanted to ask you—" his voice trailed away. "When I got
in last night, this morning, all the lights in my apartment were on.
I'd left them off, of course."

"You didn't go up by yourself," Mae breathed, pushing the pillows behind her and sitting up.

"Oh, there's nothing here worth stealing except the piano, and
a burglar would have to be out of his mind to try to get that down
the stairs. No, my son, Tim, came home in the middle of the night.
He's here now. It's rather awkward." Jason stopped, as if needing
to grope for words to explain. Into Mae's mind came the sudden
image of a mourner at a funeral who, as he walks from church,
casts a discreet eye over the congregation to gauge the impact of
his grief. Instead of irritating her, his self-consciousness was en-
dearing; she sensed his inability to call her without some grand
excuse to justify the move, and this proved at once his overwhelming pride, which she knew about, and his interest in her, which
she was only now beginning to understand.

But he was speaking. "Tim's been kicked out of school. He came
here because his mother was making calls about enrolling him in
another. We've been yelling at each other all morning. We only
stopped because I had to find a cigarette and came into my study to
get more. When I saw the phone I thought at once of calling you. I
hope you don't mind," he said, suddenly formal.

"Why was he kicked out?" Mae remembered at once what Justina had told her about Tim Dewar. A wild kid, a bad influence. A
boy from a broken home. If Danny ever called from the bus station
to tell his parents he was home from school a month early because
he had been kicked out, Daniel wouldn't let him in the house. He
would just scream at his son over the phone and leave him to figure

out his own mess.

"He got into some trouble, drugs. Three other boys were in-volved and got kicked out as well. Dumb kids. This isn't the first time for any of them. They had all been warned about drinking in the dorm. Tim had just gotten off probation for that. It was his first weekend free. The boy has absolutely no sense. I just don't understand what he was up to."

Mae heard the scrape of a match and pictured him clamping the phone between chin and shoulder while he lit another cigarette. "Look," she said hesitantly. "Would you like me to come over? Sometimes having another person around can make it easier to talk. You're less likely to go around in circles."

"Would you?" She heard the relief, and, the something else, the interest, in his voice. "I don't want to get angry at the kid, but I just can't seem to get through to him."

"I'll be over in an hour."

The phone rang again as she was buttoning her coat. "Sorry, Andy," she said. "I'm going to do this before I back out." She slammed the door on the ringing phone, then unlocked it to reach in for the pile of yesterday's mail to read in the cab.

Mae heard the piano as she climbed the stairs to Jason Dewar's apartment. It was stormy playing; chords crashed up and down the keyboard. Schumann, her teacher's mind observed, a piece from the "Fantasiestucke," and he didn't have all the notes yet. His pedalling was sloppy; he blurred phrases together; there were painful discords. Yet he played with such longing that she stopped before the door, unwilling to break into his mood, afraid, really, to enter and confront the loneliness that he was battling. She heard in his playing what he would never admit in words (a wrong note made her wince): his terrible need to be heard and understood and the fiercer pride which cloaked that need, kept him from relenting, giving in and agreeing to seek joy outside the sound which tore at him, which he tore at now as though yearning to escape.

There were hurried steps behind her. Mae turned: Jason. She should have known better than to imagine he would reveal so much of himself even in his music.

"I went out to get more coffee," he said, breathing hard. "I figured you deserved that much for coming over on such short notice to help someone you hardly know talk to his kid. You're quick getting here."

"I took a cab," Mae said. "Is that Tim playing?" She nodded toward the door.

"Yes." Jason dug keys from his jacket.

Mae laid her hand over the doorknob. "How old is he, exactly?"

"Not more than eighteen. Seventeen, I think. His birthday's in December."

"He's very good. Did you teach him?"

Jason tossed his keys from one hand to the other. "His mother insisted that he learn. She had him at the piano when he was four. Abby loved to tell people that she never had to remind him to practice; she'd find him sitting on the piano bench with his legs sticking straight out in front of him, absorbed in picking out a scale the way other boys are when they're arranging battles for their plastic soldiers." His voice was thin with irritation; the smile he'd greeted her with tensed, as he spoke, into his usual mask. As though her questions about Tim were as impertinent as some reporter's curiosity, as though she were pressing him for details on "how much practice? how long? how young?" so she could formulate a definitive theory with which to instruct her readers how they, too, might produce a prodigy. More likely, her doggedness reminded him of his ex-wife. Mae stepped back from the door so he could unlock it.

"Tim can be difficult," he warned, holding the door for her.

They stepped into the living room, pausing beside an arrangement of low chairs. The room beyond was so long and bare that Mae's eyes travelled uninterrupted to the far end where the well-polished grand piano gleamed in the light from a wall of windows. Heavy burgundy curtains were tied back on either side, so whoever sat at the piano had a partial view of the city below. All Mae saw of Tim was longish dark hair with the coarse texture of Jason's, and his back in a yellow t-shirt. He knew they were there: his shoulders stiffened, hunched, then dropped, and he switched without stopping into a simple piece, an early Bach Invention which he played woodenly from memory, his left hand making entrances in the very precise, exaggerated gestures a teacher would use to illustrate to a child how the left hand had to come in to make itself heard over the stronger right hand. Tim played very loudly.

"You plan to audition with that piece?" Jason called over the noise. He meant it as a kind of joke, Mae saw; he went on into the kitchen with the groceries, throwing the keys on a glass-topped coffeetable.

The boy jerked his hands from the keyboard. "Sorry you don't like it, Papa," accenting the last syllable with the over-exaggerated refinement that his left hand had acquired in the Bach. Then he dropped his hands again and went on with the Invention. As though, Mae thought, he could drown out our presence, as though he could play us to death.

"Coffee?" Jason yelled from the archway which separated the dining and the living rooms. Mae yelled back, "Please," and he vanished again. She moved uncertainly into the no-man's-land between the piano and the low beige armchairs, stopping in front of floor-to-ceiling shelves built into the wall which held Jason's record collection. She looked at the album covers, jamming her hands uneasily in her coat pockets. With relief she felt the crumpled envelope she had thrust there, a letter from Justina she hadn't had time to read on the ride over. Something tangible she could concentrate on while she waited for her role here to become clear.

Dear Mae, the letter began,

Just a note to remind you of our Thanksgiving plans. Mae glanced at the date. Last week. Dinner will be at 3, and we'll expect you to stay over with us. Danny's home for the break, but there's always room for you. He looks a little thin, and doesn't seem to do a thing but sleep— comes down to breakfast at noon every day!! But you know how boys are. Everybody's doing great and can't wait to see you—just like old times!! Love, Sister.

So she didn't hear a thing I told her when we talked. Mae shoved the letter back in her pocket, her impatience with Justina momentarily distracting her from the noise in the room. Tim was on another Invention now, one she'd suffered through too often at students' recitals. Tim banged out the lines of counterpoint in perfect parody of a stiff-fingered ten-year-old. She didn't understand why Jason didn't stop his son's noise. It was as if he hadn't noticed that the piano had become a weapon, that Tim was pounding out some kind of warning; it was as though he heard only the sounds of some not-very-skilled student attempting Bach. Failing at it, yes, but after all practicing, and so not to be interrupted just because that practicing annoyed you. Any more than you requested that the clarinet teacher whose office was over yours keep his students from bleating scales during your office hours. Music was music, and they had to learn to play it somewhere.

It was odd, Mae thought, her head beginning to ring with the notes which seemed to vibrate from the very floor and caused her finally to retreat to the sofa near the door, odd that none of the neighbors telephoned to stop the noise. But perhaps to them any music coming from this apartment was art and to be respected.

"There isn't any milk." Jason stood beside her with two mugs, slopping coffee onto the beige rug.

"I drank it," Tim said loudly, without turning, though he appeared to be absorbed in playing the same four-measure phrase over and over. If volume wouldn't drive them away, repetition might.

"You don't drink your coffee black. I know that much about you." Jason set the mugs down with a distracted frown. "I'll go borrow some from the landlady."

"It's all right, Jason, really. I don't mind it like this." But he had already slammed the door behind him, forgetting, her housewife mind noted, the keys. She took a sip of the coffee and set it down hastily.

In the middle of his thirty-somethingth repeat of the phrase, Tim stopped playing. He swung long legs over the piano bench and inspected her.

"You're Dann-o's aunt," he said at last.

This conjuncton of her worlds seemed no more outrageous than the complex and in the last twenty minutes deafening overlap of contrapuntal harmonies.

"How do you know Danny?"

"Elijah Bennington Hall, The Carlton School, Carlton, Connecticut," he answered promptly, intoning the address in the voice of one long-drilled in this particular exercise. His face was long-boned, already as thin as Jason's, and his eyes were fierce now with a small child's triumph of beating an adult in a game. Then as suddenly they softened. He rubbed the piano bench with strong fingers. "I saw you last year at Parents' Weekend," he admitted. "You drove up with Dann-o's mom in that new car. It was my first term, too. Dad couldn't come up, but my mom was there." He glanced at her speculatively. "Do you know her?"

"No," Mae said firmly. "Just your father. I play violin in his orchestra."

"Right." Tim gave the word all the innuendo he could muster. Then he grinned. "Too bad for you."

"Oh, it's not that awful. Your father has worked miracles with the orchestra. We can't complain about a little discipline. Maybe you'll come to one of our concerts."

"If I'm around." He said it absently. "Dann-o and I lived on the same floor. He had the single at the end of the hall. We used to fight over the bathroom mirror in the morning. Shaving." This, claimed proudly, was a clear exaggeration. "I live—lived—with three other guys. Like our own little quartet. They called us the gang of four."

"And you were all kicked out together?" she asked gently.

Tim shrugged, turning back to the piano and picking out a scale. "All four. Dann-o wasn't involved. Don't worry. He doesn't, didn't, have anything to do with our crowd. He was pretty much a recluse; he kept to himself. He's always worrying over his work. I guess his folks really put the pressure on for him to get the grades."

"They want him to do well," Mae began. The doorknob rattled. Jason yelled, "Milkman. Open up."

"You didn't have to bother," she told him, letting him in. "But thank you."

Jason brought the coffeepot and two clean cups. Mae glanced at the far end of the room. "Tim, why don't you come join us?" she called. She was surprised that he stood up right away and strolled down the long room toward them, hands in his jean pockets. Even in sock feet he was as tall as his father. "I'm sure there's enough for three," she said. Jason sank into an armchair beside the couch and let his hands drop to the floor. He said nothing.

"I'll get another cup." Tim wheeled abruptly toward the kitchen.

Jason didn't ask her about her time alone with Tim. He was remote, closed off, as though he were working out in his mind the choreography of the next encounter with his son. Mae was aware how keenly attentive he was to any sound from the kitchen: the rattle of the mug as Tim pulled it from a shelf, the slam of a cupboard door, the slow shuffle of his sock feet crossing the tile, their muffled weight on the dining room carpet. Jason shut his eyes for a moment, one hand coming up to partially shield his face. Mae sat quietly, not daring to intrude. As Tim's steps came closer, Jason sat up; as if, Mae thought, he were timing this, counting out the measures for the precise beat in which he must speak. And if he times it right, if he comes in perfectly on cue, whatever he says will sound natural and right and captivate his audience, his son.

Tim sat on the arm of the sofa opposite Mae.

"Not on the arm, Tim. You know you're too heavy to sit there," Jason snapped. His son slid instantly to the floor and wrapped his legs around the legs of the coffee table, locking his hands together on the glass top. There was a long silence.

"It's a lovely piano," Mae ventured. "The bass is clear and not too heavy."

"We've always had it. It was my first investment when I started earning money from conducting. It's been moved around more than is really good for it. But I'd hate to give it up, all the same. I guess I'm like a miser with his first nickel."

"Why give it up? It's still a good piano," Tim burst out, as if defending the fate of an aging pet.

"Is it the one you learned on?" Mae asked him.

Tim laughed, a quick, ugly sound. Jason shook his head and reached for a cigarette from a wooden box on the table. "Tim wasn't allowed to touch it until he was ten. I didn't want him playing on it before I was sure he was old enough to respect it. A Chickering grand isn't something you want a kid banging around on." Absorbed in lighting his cigarette, he didn't notice the look Tim shot him, resentment, just as quickly shut away. Mae felt herself in the middle of an old, old battle which she didn't know how to head off.

"Mom used to open it for me when you were off on tour. I wasn't supposed to tell you about it. She said I ought to know what it was like to play on a decent instrument, not that old upright you had put in my nursery."

Jason breathed long around his cigarette. When he spoke his

voice was tight but controlled. "Your mother and I disagreed on a number of things. One of which was the best manner in which to bring you up. If she had had her way, you both would have traipsed around the country after me, hopping from city to city, living in hotel rooms, moving on every few weeks like migrant workers."

Tim grinned. "How many migrant workers did you meet in those hotels of yours, Pop?"

"Tim." Jason sounded tired. "You know what I mean. I wanted you to get a solid education at a good school."

Tim kicked at a far leg of the table. "Much good as school has done me, I might as well have followed around after you. I would have learned something about music, and you and Mom might have gotten to know each other a little better."

"What your mother and I know about one another is none of your damn business," Jason shot at him. "You would have learned something worthwhile if you could have stayed in one school for more than a year at a time."

"I'd be dead by now if I'd stayed at any of those places longer than I did. When are you going to understand that the schools you send me to have nothing to do with the kind of person I am, with the kind of thing I want to do?" Tim sprang to his feet and began circling the group of chairs in a frantic pacing. His eyes never left his father. "When are you going to admit what I am? I'm not a scholar. I'm never going to be. I'm not any good with books or writing papers. I hate sitting around talking about ideas." He drawled the word to absurdity. "Those everlasting class discussions of great books make me sick. All the guys scoring points off each other, but politely, men; always speak politely." Tim gasped for breath. "And I hate running around the soccer field while some coach yells at me to run faster. When are you going to let me do what I want to do?"

"You're too young to know what you want to do. I've said this again and again. You need a broader background before you can make that sort of decision."

"You're afraid I'll fail." Tim stopped pacing and looked coldly down at his father. Jason's hand clenched against the arm of his chair. Here it comes, thought Mae. After a morning of yelling at one another about bad habits, dangerous influences, credits lost, tuition wasted, they were down to what mattered, to what would wound more than all that ritual circling around past failures.

"It's true." His voice was taunting now, with the desperate fury of a child who must wound quickly before he is sent or dragged off to his room, a tantrum his only defense against forces beyond his control. "I used to think you didn't want me to be a musician because that was what Mom wanted for me. I hated you for that, for the way you always left us behind. But it wasn't that, it wasn't that at all." He lowered his voice, seeing from his father's face that what he said hurt more than his manner of saying it. "You were afraid I couldn't live up to your name." The words tore from him with a raw edge of wonder that they could hurt so much. "You didn't want me to have your name. Mother said you didn't want me to be a second Jason Dewar; you didn't want another Jason Dewar. You didn't want to share any part of yourself with me. You had so many excuses. You had to study a new score; you had to go off to rehearsal; you had to work until a piece was perfect, or there was no point in playing it at all. I should have known then that you would never want me to have a part of your precious music, either."

"It's such an awful life, Tim."

Mae heard the pleading in Jason's voice. His face was grey, his hands shaking as after a performance. They couldn't keep on like this. She turned and touched Tim's shoulder.

"It can be terribly lonely, Tim. There's so much work before you can perform, and once you do, you never know how it will go the next time." She knelt on her chair so that she faced Jason, keeping her hand on Tim's arm. "But it is his life, Jason, awful or not. He has to decide for himself."

Beneath the hand which shaded his eyes, Jason nodded.

Tim moved around Mae's chair to stand before his father, his arms spread wide. "I know it's going to be hard. I know all about that. Do you think, Pa, that I didn't see how late you had to work? Some nights when I'd go down to the kitchen for a drink, your study door would be open and you'd still be sitting there in that old brown armchair with scores spread across your lap and on the floor. I know it's not going to stop, all the preparation. I know I'll have to study and study. And I know how far I am from the point that I can even begin to claim to be a musician. But I will be." Jason took his hand from his face. "I will be. I hear music the way you do. And that's not something that will stop just because you would prefer I do something else with my life."

He stuck his hands back in his pockets and rocked back and forth on his heels.

"It's your life," Jason said, not ironically, not unkindly.

After a few moments Tim went to the piano and quietly began a Chopin nocturne. He let the seven-note pattern in the bass dominate, the repeated rhythm holding the melody immobile, so that instead of the bittersweet rushing treble Mae heard the repetition, and felt the three of them bound in a stillness where nothing would change. Gradually, as Tim forgot about the two who listened behind him, the music took over and the nocturne swept ahead into its intended passion. But for one moment, there had been rest.

They ate a late lunch in front of a small fire that Tim built. As they sipped hot soup, Tim talked: it was all settled; everything was going to work out great. He wouldn't waste any more time in boarding school. He'd get an audition and get into one of the good conservatories. Maybe Curtis. He would stay there for two years, and then get some kind of scholarship to study abroad with a really good teacher. Later on, he would come back to the States to play, perhaps to teach. At seventeen, thought Mae, it must all seem so clear, the milestones of applications and acceptances jutting out straight and clean and easily overcome, no inkling yet of those unexpected details which would muddle that open, wide sweep to the horizon where his future lay. She remembered the overwhelming confidence with which she had glided through her eighteenth year: rules were for adults to pay heed to, already stuck as they were in petty daily doings where traffic laws and taxes and insurance were things to worry over. Nothing would get in her way; life waited on her to move through it. She had been buoyant and joyous and full of faith in her own ability.

And for Tim, it might work out that way. Now, bent over the piano, his face was relaxed and purposeful. He had asked his father for advice on the best phrasing in the sonata. Jason sat beside him on the piano bench and played the line one way, and then another, offering them without comment for Tim to choose from. The reading lamp cast their reflections sharply against the dark November evening in the wall of windows. Mae, on the couch, fought against envy. Tim was going to have such an easy time! While she, Andy, so many others, had struggled so long alone before daring to ask for help, to admit to anyone else what they wanted. Not to mention the ones like Danny, who couldn't even begin to articulate what they wanted from life.

"Any guess what Danny will wind up doing?" she had asked Justina as they washed dishes after Christmas dinner last year. She had hoped to hit on a subject which her sister would relax with; Justina had seemed particularly tense the whole holiday, and for some reason, all the more so throughout the meal.

"Your guess is as good as mine." Justina's laugh had been brittle, and Mae's heart sank. "His father expects he'll go on to graduate school, of course, as though that's the ultimate solution. Take out another student loan and keep reading books. No mention of how Danny ought to start planning how he's going to look after himself when he's through with all this schooling. But then Daniel doesn't concern himself with that sort of minor detail. It clutters up the scholar's mind, I suppose. He certainly doesn't have the least idea what his son is interested in doing."

Do you? Mae had wondered silently. She opened cupboard doors, trying to figure out where Justina kept the good china saucers.

"Over the stove," Justina told her. "No, Daniel's in a little world of his own, and his children will just have to get along as they can."

It wasn't that she wished on Tim a more difficult time, Mae thought. It was just that his luck, the apparent ease with which he was moving into his career without agonizing over whether it was right or wrong, startled her into wondering all sorts of what if's. What if someone in her family had been a musician or even musical, what might she have been encouraged to go on and become? Instead of this, being just ordinary, using her small given talent to keep up with rent payments.

But that was sinking into herself, and she had long ago resolved not to allow herself that indulgence. Justina brooded over the past, wondered why this had happened to her instead of that, where she had gone wrong, and Justina asked her wistfully over the phone, "Are YOU happy?" Mae refused that trap. Anyway, she had a schedule full of students in the morning and Andy to talk to, and Tim said goodnight to her with a quiet, "Danny's lucky," which sent her straight back to the night years ago when she had been in the boys' room singing them to sleep and a chunky five-year-old Nathan interrupted her rendition of "Oh Danny Boy" to ask "Aren't there any songs you can sing about a Nathan boy?" And Jason Dewar insisted on walking out with her to find her a cab, and shut her safely inside, then leaned on the window to thank her again for coming over. "Just thought I better warn you," he ended. "I'd like to see you again." She hadn't imagined that.

Mae opened her eyes and was awake at once. Rather, her eyelids sprang apart while every other muscle tensed to listen like an animal, big-eyed, crouched in the forest. With effort she kept her eyes from darting side to side, afraid the faint twitch would alert whatever it was that she had heard that she was awake. She stared until she felt her eyes strain in their sockets. But she could distinguish nothing in the soft blackness of the room.

Of course, it might have been some sudden noise from downstairs. Mrs. Ferguson sometimes shrieked her husband's name and then fell silent, her rage apparently spent. Perhaps she had thrown something at him just now, a shoe, a book, a knife. Mae let her breath out and stared not quite so intently around. One sound resolved itself into the soft whirr of the refrigerator; another was the companionable rattle of air in the radiator pipes. It was so quiet that she felt she could almost catch the bump of the moths as they flung themselves against the streetlight below her window.

There it was again. Mae's heart whipped her blood to jelly that surged to her throat and down to her toes, rendering her limp with fear. A noise as it were glimpsed out of the corner of the eye, as when a leaf flutters past the window and you look up in time to see the tip of it disappear or notice some disturbance in the air. Yet sight, Mae believed, plays a hundred tricks. The shadow you swear you saw move may be nothing more than the fall of your own eyelash. While sound, either you heard a thing or you didn't; there could be no imagining it; you couldn't black out what was there.

If for some reason she couldn't hear a sound which she knew had been made, her mind supplied the noise—when the glass of the window kept her from hearing the splash of rain into a puddle on the sidewalk, her ear recreated the sound of the drop bursting into the surface of the water. Then there was the noise of dreams: Andy told her you never dreamed in sound. Yet, she sometimes woke up because someone was calling to her. "Mae. May-ay."

She knew she'd heard something. There must be something there.

The very absence, now, of sound was proof to her that there had been something. It was too still, as if something in this room held its breath; someone.

Mae breathed in a slow careful rhythm to make it sound as though she slept. There was no noise, but she was aware that something solid, some thing, had shifted towards her.

"Please." She spoke suddenly. "Take whatever you want. The silver is in the kitchen. The stereo is in the living room. There are some good records. The only jewelry I have is in the top drawer of my dresser. My pearls. They were my mother's, they're real. And my watch, it's on top, you can have that, too. I haven't got any money here. Take what you want, but please, leave me alone."

She shouldn't plead with him. "There are people right below here who can hear everything that goes on in this apartment."

She waited for an answer, tensing herself for the clatter of her belongings as they were scraped into a sack. But he didn't move. Surely there was nothing there. Except that over by the window, beside the dresser, Mae could swear that there was something in the darkness that was solid, dark, that had substance. It was some-time later that she knew that whatever had been there was gone. Whatever it was had withdrawn silently, melted away, simply dis-solved into the thinner darkness of the room.

All next day, she was lightheaded and jittery with sleepless-ness and the coffee she kept drinking to pull herself awake for the students who came in a steady stream for their lessons. As if in conspiracy, none of them were prepared.

"Did you even practice this?" she asked Melissa Watson, know-ing that Mrs. Watson would call her up at supper time and demand to know why it was necessary to snap at her child. After Kenneth stumbled three times on the first line of his Mozart, she pulled the music off the stand. "You sound like you're sight-reading," she told him. "I guess you're not ready for this piece after all." He refused to look at her for the rest of the lesson, and, when the phone rang, sidled out of the apartment without saying goodbye.

It was Jason. "I thought you'd like to know that Tim got an audition for Curtis," he said. "They want him to play for them next week. He's practiced all afternoon."

Yes, yes; Mae brushed the news aside into the confusion that was her tired mind grappling with the day and last night's intrusion. Of course Tim would get things as he wanted them. He always would. She realized that Jason was waiting for some response.

"That's great."

Jason's voice burst in too quickly to cover the silence. "Well, I didn't mean to interrupt you in the middle of your students, I just wanted to share the good news with you, since you were trapped in the middle of us yesterday."

"Of course. I'm glad you called." She wasn't. She couldn't tell him about last night, and that was all she could think about right now. And the fact that she couldn't tell him rose between them as an impassable barrier: she knew something was in the way; he sensed it; neither could mention it, and he hung up with a decided reserve in his farewell.

The student whose lesson followed Kenneth's didn't show up and didn't call to explain and didn't answer when she called him, so that Mae spent the better part of the next hour wandering around her apartment wondering what had happened to him, before deciding to salvage the time by writing to Justina. She ruined two postcards of Boston Common snowscenes before she managed a note which didn't sound irritable.

> Justina— she wrote.
> You're sweet to want to include me in your Thanksgiving plans but I honestly couldn't make it down. I know you're having a lovely time. Tell Danny I still want him to visit, and hope he will come sometime soon.
> xxx Mae,

which was all the encouragement she dared to send to Danny at home. Anything more Justina would interpret as interference, and a letter to him would create so much curiosity that it was better to send none at all. She stared for a long time at her pen, envisioning a letter which he could turn to again and again for encouragement. She could send it to school, and he'd get it as soon as he got back. But she couldn't settle down to write it, and finally went into the kitchen to fix lunch.

"Damn them all!" Mae whacked the soup spoon hard against the pot she stirred, splattering drops of tomato red across the stove. "Let them look after themselves then."

That night, she simply woke and knew. There was someone close beside her bed. She knew this as clearly as you know someone at the next table is staring at you as if he wants to know you.

Slowly she turned her head towards him, conscious of the loud rasp of her hair against the pillow. There was no definite outline to indicate how tall, how broad, no details to suggest how old, just a kind of thicker blackness against the dark of the room.

He wasn't going to hurt her. She sensed that as surely as she sensed his presence. So the throb of terror she felt on opening her eyes dropped away. He was there. But what was he going to do?

Mae stared at him until her eyes began to blur the tones of black that distinguished him from the other dark shapes in the room: the squat low bulk of the dresser, the thin angled slant of her closet door, the twin spikes of the bedposts, her robe draped over the left one. He never moved. Yet his very presence demanded something of her, some response. She began to feel like he was someone she knew, patiently waiting there for her to wake up. I believe in all things, seen and unseen, she thought, then fought against this calm acceptance. He couldn't be there. No one could break into an apartment so quietly; no one could stand there without moving for so long. He couldn't be real.

He never moved, and so comfortable had Mae become in his presence that without willing it, she fell asleep.

"You look tired," Andy told her. They had finished lunch and were sunning in a quiet corner of the university campus, sitting on a low brick wall with their backs to the small fountain it encircled. The water was turned off for the winter, though the day was as balmy as mid-March, with fat clouds rolling together overhead and crumpled brown leaves scudding past like kites.

"I've been staying up late to practice." Mae stubbornly pushed aside the temptation to confide in Andy. She hadn't told Jason about her dream-visitant; she wouldn't say anything to Andy. She wasn't confused by what she had seen any more, but she didn't have words to describe it. If she tried, he might try to laugh her out of taking it so seriously, and she wasn't ready yet to lose the mystery; she didn't want it translated, explained away in everyday terms. In this bright winter light where the difference between subject and shadow was as stark as black silhouettes pasted onto white paper, where the black tree limbs stood clearly against the pale sky, it would be all too easy for Andy to persuade her that what she saw at night was illusion. Talking about it now would be like describing moonbeams while under the glare of fluorescent light.

Andy lay back on his elbows, his head tipped back to the sky. Mae shifted her weight to her left hand, flinging the other impatiently towards the dry fountain. She didn't want to relax back into the certain intimacy of Andy's company. She wanted to push forward, push beyond, forge a new kinship. Jason Dewar; the name started a curl of impatience in her stomach. Why hadn't he called since Monday? Was he ever going to call with anything other than Tim to talk about? Would he ever ask her why she looked so tired, and how was she really doing, anyway?

"This fountain looks pretty depressing," Andy said idly. He rolled his head back to focus on Mae. "You've got circles under your eyes. You know better than to let a performance get you uptight."

"I'm not worried about the quartet." Her voice had the thin, stretched quality of something about to break, but Andy appeared to notice only the words.

"Well, that's good. We've played the Dissonant until I hear discord in my dreams." At her exclamation, he sat up and laid his hand against the back of her neck. She flung it off and stood, glaring at him.

"Sorry." He held his hands up in surrender. Mae ignored him

and began to pace around the fountain. Bits of candy wrapper foil and plastic ice cream spoons littered the cement circle. Of course, no one had bothered to clean up the trash. She could just see the kind of people who left such a mess behind, completely self-absorbed, eager to gobble down their chocolate, let the paper fall where it would, or, giddy with the pleasure of love and ice cream, dropping their garbage behind.

"Everything is so ugly!" she cried, kicking at the bench chained to the ground. Paint peeled from its seat in long green strips exposing the yellow wood beneath. "There's nothing in this whole city with any gracefulness or meaning. Nobody cares about anything but themselves. It's all do-what-you-can-for-yourself, and let the rest go to hell." She refused to cry. She paced back to the fountain. "I wish!" she cried, pulling from the pockets of her tan raincoat bits of kleenex and a broken violin string and, finally, a handful of change which she flung onto the dry bed of the little fountain, "I wish something mattered!"

Andy took her by the shoulders. "Mae. You walk past this, past worse than this every day and it never bothers you. You usually don't even notice. What's wrong?"

"Nothing." Her throat was tight.

"Nothing that you're going to tell me."

She shrugged. She ought to tell him and get over it, let the mysterious uneasiness which rose in her at the thought of her intruder or dream or whatever it was be reduced through words to a manageable problem with a logical explanation.

"It's been a long week," she said.

Andy pulled her arm through his. "Tell you what. Let's get away from this place. There's a trio recital at the music building this afternoon. I used to know the cellist. They ought to give a decent performance. Maybe they'll restore your faith in the potential of the human race."

"I ought to get home." She let him lead her out of the courtyard back to the main quadrangle of the campus where students hurried past with faces anxiously turned toward the library, finals coming up in two weeks. "I'm expecting a phone call."

"Right." Andy walked faster. "No one of any importance calls you except me. This is music, girl, and you're in the music business. Come on."

She was going to hate the concert. It was going to be awful. The boxy new recital hall gleamed of white paint and light-polished wood, like the sanctuary of the church she had attended with her family so long ago. Sound would bounce and shatter like crystal on the shining surfaces. There was no softness anywhere to muffle a missed note, no stage curtains, no carpet in the aisles.

"These acoustics won't forgive a thing," Mae said. "They'd better be awfully good."

Andy ignored her and led the way down the aisle. Straight-backed wooden chairs balanced on thin legs in rigid lines across the floor.

"We're not going to be able to see," Mae said to Andy's back. She didn't even notice that he led them to seats on the left side of the stage, thus violating their old, just and never-broken custom of sitting stage-right before intermissions so Andy could be closer to the cellist. After intermissions they moved stage-left for Mae.

"How's this?" Andy waited for her near the front.

"Whatever." Mae shrugged. They had to climb over the feet and knapsacks of several students to reach their seats. The hall was full of students, popping up to call to friends in the back, kneeling backwards in their seats to examine the crowd behind them. Mae glared at one girl who stood in front of the stage conducting an extended conversation with someone in the back of the hall. The full tunic she wore over tight black slacks was belted around an impossibly tiny waist. No student should have time to look that fashionable. Mae was certain that this was one of the girls who hung over Jason after rehearsals. Surely he was able to tell from the way she flung herself around that her prime interest in life did not lie in analyzing his orchestration.

In front of Andy, two carefully tousled hair-dos bobbed together and then apart in an endless toss and shiver of thick light hair. Mae refused to believe that the two girls were engaged in so intense a discussion that it required them to lean together and then start apart with such shaking of the head. Don't strain yourselves, girls, she wanted to tell them, it's only me back here.

"You're steaming, Mae," Andy said, without looking up from the program he studied.

"These are the musicians of the future? Well, thank god for old recordings." She watched a boy with baby-plump cheeks lean towards the two blondes, his full lips almost quivering in his eagerness to talk. At least he's got the vocabulary down pat, Mae thought, as snatches of the conversation rose over the scrape of chairs against the floorboards. Lyricism; subdominant; the ultimate recording. The darker of the girls turned her head so that Mae couldn't help but see every muscle of her velvet-eyelashed profile tense and relax as she chewed several pieces of gum. "God," she said, with an especially loud snap, "there's old Do-it-himself. God, he's gorgeous." Her friend turned to look, ignoring the boy who babbled on beside them. Some suspicion made Mae glance over her shoulder. Jason Dewar stood in the rear aisle surveying the crowd. He looked very European, very much the conductor, in a dark turtleneck and muted tweed jacket. He turned to someone behind him, his face opening in a smile that hit Mae like a blast of cold air. Who was with him?

The girls tossed their heads together and apart once more. "But I've never *seen* him smile like that," Mae heard. She pleated her program into a fan, then twisted that to shreds.

"It looks like a good concert," Andy said. "They're doing the Mendelssohn."

She shouldn't be here. She should be home, outside, anywhere but in this tiny hall hemmed in by students who glowed with confidence. She was invisible, a nonentity. If she slid to the floor and disappeared, no one would notice. It wasn't fair. She was everyone's ear. Jussie, Jason, everyone turned to her when they needed help. "You're such a good listener," a student's mother had told her after a long monologue which began as an inquiry into her daughter's behavior during lessons and ended, some forty-five minutes later, as a desperate recital of her own depression. "I feel better just talking to you. You ought to be a counsellor." Which was, Mae understood, the woman's vocabulary for anyone receptive and sensitive and mostly patient enough to listen and occasionally interject advice. In other words, a friend. "I'm a musician," Mae told her. "I make my living by my ear." But no one ever listened to her. Mae stared hard at the stage, blinking back tears.

"Either tell me what's wrong or don't, but don't sit there and get mad at the music," Andy hissed into her ear. Mae swallowed hard. Andy, yes Andy would listen, but he was not the audience she wanted.

Two men and a woman with a cello had walked onto the stage. The woman arranged with one quick practiced flip the long full folds of her divided skirt and settled the cello closer to her. Mae concentrated fiercely on their first phrases, hoping by the effort of analyzing what she heard to avoid the bleakness which washed over her. But their playing was shallow, sloppy. As though to make up for their poor playing, the three were in continual motion, bending or swaying. The violinist grimaced before every long run; the pianist attacked chords with a flourish of his elbows like a bird swelling its wings. Someone gasped for breath before each downbeat. Mae gave up trying to listen and sank into a bitter silence from which she felt she would never escape.

At the intermission, talk and laughter rose in waves around her. Andy was speaking with one of the faculty. Mae almost clenched her teeth to keep from flinging her head back, flailing her fists like a child, and crying, "Why not me?" In reality she sat beside Andy, her face like a stone.

"I've got to get out of here," she managed to whisper to Andy, and pushed her way out to the aisle. She felt his hand on her shoulder. "I'm sorry," she said. "I just can't take any more."

"They were pretty disappointing. We don't have to stay for the rest." As he reached for the door, it was pulled open from the outside, and Mae, who had automatically stepped forward, ran headlong into Tim Dewar.

"Hi," he said, moving back to let her pass. His smile faded as she stepped sideways onto the porch, her hand in Andy's. He jerked his head at his father, who was stubbing a cigarette into the stone railing. "Come on, Dad, we might lose our seats."

"Surely not." Jason patted his pockets for his cigarettes, then looked up to see Mae. He smiled and seemed ready to speak, but Tim's voice pulled him along. "You don't need to smoke anymore, Dad. Let's go."

"Enjoy the concert," Andy said. Jason raised a hand to them and followed his son inside.

"Not one of your conquests, that boy."

"I don't understand," Mae looked after them with a puzzled expression. "We talked for hours just a few days ago. I don't get it." All the while relief sang in her: he had been with Tim, no one else.

"I guess it doesn't do to look too closely into the workings of the adolescent mind. I'll walk you home."

Mae raced back downstairs. Andy had to still be there. The call hadn't been that long. She searched the street as if the urgency of her need might have somehow frozen time so she would see his long lean raincoated back proceeding nonchalantly to the corner.

But while she had been on the phone, night had fallen; Andy was long gone. The lights of a car rounding the corner fixed on the dark skeleton of a tree which grew in the sidewalk. In the double shaft of light which quivered as if alive, mist danced. The car turned and sped by with a shriek. Mae plunged down the sidewalk after it, the sound of her rapid footsteps reverberating in the tunnel of apartment building walls. The car disappeared around the block and Mae slowed, the words jerked from her with every gasp for breath. "Not Danny. Not my Danny."

She walked to escape the sound. On the street parallel to her own, people pushed past, hurrying to late elegant dinners out or theatre seats. Mae focused on keeping out of their way. How many times she had rushed along this sidewalk in her black concert dress, legs trembling with the urgency to be on time. Tonight she let these anxious ones bump her about like a leaf rushed along a stream, twisted and turned until the weight of some random spray of water ducks it under for the last time.

Only by walking faster and faster could she calm the words that spun around her brain: Danny was dead and she had never helped him.

On the phone with Daniel she kept asking, when? When did it

happen? like any other relative groping for a response to tragedy and preferring to grapple with the facts of when and where and how than attempt to understand the why.

Yet it seemed important that she know when. If it had happened on the night that she had first been wakened—Mae's conscious mind rebelled, and she heard herself repeating, "Where was he? How did he do it?"

Daniel's voice plodded on through a myriad of unrelated detail. "We had picked him up a few nights before. It was his Thanksgiving vacation. He had the whole week off. Most schools just have two days. He was supposed to bring home his books to study for finals, but he didn't have one of them. The Cavins were all driving over for Thanksgiving dinner. They hadn't seen him for months. I don't know what we'll do with all the food Justina fixed. All kinds of stuff. I guess it'll freeze. Or we may need it for the funeral."

"When will that be?"

"We won't tell the grandparents what happened, of course. Papaw Cavin is pushing ninety. We told them what we told everybody outside the immediate family. Danny was killed in a car accident. He was out driving late at night in a car he borrowed from a friend, something he had no business doing, but it would be just like him. There's no reason for the whole world to know what happened. We can spare him that."

And keep the family honor untarnished, Mae added silently.

"There are a lot of people who think highly of Danny. For his sake we don't want them to have to change their opinions."

Mae swallowed the bitterness which caught like bile in her throat. "When was this, Daniel?"

"I was working in my office at the university when Justina called. Normally, I would never stay so late at night but it's difficult to write at home when Danny's back from school." His voice caught and snagged on his son's name, despite himself. Mae wished she could feel sorrier for him, but her grief was all for Danny, home on vacation and knowing he disrupted the way things ought to be.

"I don't think he ever appreciated the opportunities he had."

Mae finally got from Daniel the details of what had happened, but still she couldn't match the night Danny had died with the night she had first wakened to find—what?—in her room. She couldn't remember what night that had been. It was as if her mind refused to involve itself in this, refused to let her calculate whether or not the event had significance. Mae had told Daniel goodbye, then stood with her hand on the phone, unwilling to put it down and take the first step away. When she moved, the full searing comprehension of what they had lost would begin to blur; Danny would disappear in the arrangements she must make to go south to help bury him, and the process of smoothing away the gap left among them would begin. She owed him, at least, some moments of unmitigated pain.

The hope that Andy might still be nearby had roused her and she had run out after him, and now she stood at a five-way intersection with no clear idea of how she had gotten there or where she was. Over waves of traffic she heard the yells of a man selling newspapers behind her. He shook the pockets of his leather apron at passersby as though the jingle of real money would lure them to buy. Beside him, a convenience market let out blasts of warmed air and the odor of spoiling meat as its door opened and shut on parka-bundled students. Mae pulled the sleeves of her sweater over her hands. All she had in her skirt pocket was her keys. She didn't have enough change to call Andy, let alone to sit down some place warm and have a cup of coffee. She didn't recognize any of the shops around her, guessing only, by the number of open bookstores, that she was somewhere near the university.

The crowd behind her surged forward, pushing her to the edge of the curb. Mae had to lean back to keep from falling into the street. Inches away, cars pressed bumper to bumper to get through the light, edged onto the crosswalk to await the next green. The crowd swelled again and crossed the street, carrying Mae along. In panic, she turned and tried to push her way back to the sidewalk. Someone seized her arm.

"You trying to get trampled to death?"

"Tim!" Relief, gratitude at a familiar face made her clutch at his coat. He dropped her arm abruptly as they reached the opposite sidewalk.

"What are you doing out here by yourself? Where's your boyfriend?"

She couldn't mistake the taunting in his voice. Mae moved

closer so that they wouldn't be jostled apart. "Tim, please. I don't
know what you're thinking of me, but I've got to say this. Your
father and I—the most time I've ever spent with him was when the
three of us were at your apartment. I like him, but—boyfriend—
you'd have to have a pretty good imagination to call him that." She
could keep her voice steady, but she couldn't control the wobbling
of her chin. She put her hand over her mouth and spoke, very
quickly. "Anyway, I don't think your father would find the idea very
funny." She rubbed furiously at the tears which leaked from the
corners of her eyes.

"I didn't mean—" Tim began. "I wasn't—. I didn't mean Dad."
He stopped. "Look, you'd better come home with me. You must
be freezing." He gripped her upper arm and marched her in the
other direction. The wind stung the salted hollows at her temples
where the tears ran.

He settled her into the armchair before a fire he miraculously
contrived, then left her with a mug of steaming coffee, muttering
that he had to take care of some things. It seemed only a few
minutes later that Jason leaned over her chair and she was crying
into the rough smoky tweed of his coat.

"I was down at the department listening to a new recording," he
told her, much later. "Trying to get the noise of that awful concert
out of my ears. Tim called and told me to get my rear in gear and
get home."

Mae laughed shakily. "I'm glad you came." Her whole body felt
light, glass-fragile.

"Do you want to tell me now?"

It was not so hard, looking into his steady eyes, to finish the
story about Danny.

She let them look after her, that night. The three of them sat
before the fire, sipping sherry and hot coffee, listening to the bittersweet melody of a Shostakovich violin concerto which Tim chose.
When one record ended, he put on another. There was a continu-
ous stream of music so they didn't have to talk. Later, Tim played
for them; Mae, listening, remembered with a faint horror the resentment she had once felt for this boy, that he should have it so
easy, that he should know what it was he wanted and know how
to go about getting it. Poor Danny. But, Mae thought, her head on

Jason's shoulder, Tim had the gift, and a special shining sureness of it that nothing could tarnish. The fact that he was Jason Dewar's son would make it easier for him, yes, but the gift was his. "He's good," she whispered to Jason. "He's very good."

She must have fallen asleep to Tim's playing, for when she opened her eyes, the room was dark and quiet except for a faint hissing from the dying fire. Someone had tucked a quilt around her and taken off her shoes. As she lay looking around the unfamiliar room, she became aware of a presence which was not stereo cabinet or flare of curtain. "Jason?" she whispered. But she knew it wasn't, and, even as she spoke, was filled with a sleepy joy and relief that he had found her in this new place.

"Danny," she said. "It's all right. It will be all right. I'll take care of them." As daylight came, what had been shadow took on form and line and detail; the low mass of black against the window became Tim's piano, the lump on the floor, Jason's overcoat. Mae lay still, knowing what she had to do and why.

NATHAN HAD INTENDED to walk only as far as the clump of bushes which curved like a friendly arm around their campsite. But in his hurry to seize the berries which grew just beyond his reach and then to get the blacker ones beyond those, he pushed on and on. Berries he had torn his hands to get were spilling over the top of the plastic bowl before he looked up. The bushes were taller than he was, here. He had no idea which direction he had come from.

"Aunt Mae," he shouted. "Mom." His voice sounded awkward in the early morning quiet. But he shouted again. He even called for his sister LeeLee, who had flopped back over on her stomach when he suggested a hike after breakfast.

"Go by yourself," she had told him. "I want to finish reading my book."

"Aw, c'mon. We won't go far."

"No," she said. "Leave me alone. Mom, make him leave me alone."

"I thought we were all supposed to be doing stuff together on this trip," he railed at them both. "I thought that was the whole point of coming out here."

"Mom!" LeeLee wailed, without losing her place on the page.

"Nathan, just find something to do and go do it." His mother finished stacking the plastic cups which were spotted with orange juice and began gathering up the silverware.

"Leave the table, Jussie," Aunt Mae said. "This is your vacation,

127

remember. Come sit still. Just sit and talk." She settled herself in a lawn chair, snapping her rubber sandal against one bare heel with, to Nathan, an irritating authority. Perhaps it irritated his mother, too, for she ignored Mae's outstretched hand.

"I'll just clear things up a little, first," she said brightly. "It won't take but a minute." His mother scooped plates from the picnic table into a trash bag and gave Nathan one long I-told-you-to-find-something-to-do look before she eased into a chair beside her sister.

Nathan had scowled at LeeLee, who was still reading, and grabbed one of his mother's precious Tupperware bowls to go after blackberries before the aching inside started up again.

"Mom!" he shouted. He cupped one hand to his mouth to make the sound carry further. They've probably gone on to the lake without me, he thought. They'll never hear me from there.

He turned and began trampling down a new path through the weeds. He held the berries over his head so he wouldn't lose any more than he already had, and scrutinized the ground in front for snakes. When a briar caught his jeans, he bent and carefully worked them loose. His school jeans; Mom would be furious if he tore them. She said her fingers got enough exercise typing all day without having to sew up every hole he felt like making. He and LeeLee had learned to go easy on things like clothes since she had started working.

He couldn't see much through the thick leaves. A few bees rose angrily as he pushed against their branches. A horsefly circled his head, waiting to land and sting. Far above, a line of trees belted the gully, promising shade from the sun that streamed through these bushes. Their campsite was somewhere in those trees. The tent where Mom and Aunt Mae slept was pitched under an oak. LeeLee had complained the first night that acorns dug into her back. Last night they had lain awake together and watched the trees bending in the moonlight. They hadn't talked much; certainly they hadn't talked about what his mother still referred to as "Danny's acci-dent." But lying in a darkness that seemed to stretch over the whole world, yet held them close together, he had felt less responsible for everything. He felt safe. He even began to drift into a dream where his family was all right after all.

When the bushes clumped before him in an impassable thicket, he scolded himself. I'm not going the right way. Nathan allowed the first panic to ripple over him like a touch of sunshine on a February afternoon. He savored the shiver of fear, storing it up to recollect later when he would step safely over the bag of charcoal near their campstove. Once, entering the hallway at home after sledding for hours with Danny in snow-bleached sunlight, he had been unable to see anything. He had stumbled over somebody's shoe and kept himself from falling only by clutching onto the coat rack, which trembled with his weight. He had peered hopelessly into darkness. I am blind, he said, enjoying the thrill of horror. Eventually, of course, his eyes had adjusted to the light. Framed in the kitchen doorway, Danny was pulling off his boots. His dark hair stuck up in wet spikes, and Mom was lecturing him for forgetting to wear his cap. Nathan had shut his eyes and repeated, blind, and, for one moment, recreated that blank terror of stepping forward with no certainty of where the next foot might place him.

Well, I can go left for a little ways. I'll still be heading for the trees. It'll make a good story to tell, that I almost let a maze of bushes fool me. Like the myth with the minotaur that Danny read.

Nathan walked sideways to lessen the impact of the briars. The sun was getting hot on his head. He hoped he wouldn't wind up in some strange campsite. He didn't want anyone guiding him back. Once he was on the camp road he would be fine. The wooden signboard with "tent campers only" in yellow paint was one curve and several pine trees from their site. Site number thirty-two. He didn't need anybody's help.

Trees were before him, cool and green on the horizon, circling the gully just as the bushes circled him. But if the trees stood in a circle, which were the ones he was supposed to head for? Nathan turned in the narrow clearing he had trampled, scanning the branches above for some mark which would tell him which were the leaves he had listened to as he fell asleep last night. It was like searching the crowd in a football stadium for a face he wasn't quite sure he had ever seen.

"Aunt Mae!" he yelled. "Mom!" When his voice faded away, the sleepy drone of locusts rose around him.

The panic came again, more insistently. This time he didn't encourage it, didn't want to probe it with his tongue for the pleasure of a new taste.

"Which way?" he cried, as if the bushes that were shut against him would open up in answer.

"Danny, which way do I go?"

There was a rustling in the weeds beside his ankle, and he threw himself into the thicket opposite, fighting the branches which scraped at his face and pulled at his shirt, kicking his sneakers free of roots which grabbed at his feet. The locusts were suddenly quiet, silenced by the sound of a body thrashing through their weeds. Nathan heard only the rhythm of his breath, which fought through the baked air as a swimmer claws his way to the surface of the water.

When he had been much younger, so much younger that he couldn't recall that he actually had an age, he had been playing in some weeds behind their house. Someone started screaming and didn't stop. He remembered, or had been told the story so many times that he thought he remembered, that it was his mother who was screaming. She had looked out the kitchen window to see him playing there next to a copperhead, they said. Then he remembered standing in the shade on the porch, one finger in his mouth, the other hand clutching a shapeless stuffed teddy bear inherited from Danny who by age eight was already too old for such comforts. The colored lady who came in once a week to do the ironing stood behind him. Her hands moved gently on his head. "La, la," she said, over and over as they watched together. Even then he knew, though it took him many years to remember it, that it was not fear of the snake that held him still on the porch before a woman whose dark bulk and smell and incomprehensible language awed him, but the screaming, on and on, that pinned him there to listen to the angry grunts of men who beat with rakes and shovels the thing which writhed on the ground. Their mystical choreography reappeared in his dreams, those figures circling their victim, the inner circle with arms swinging up and more relentlessly down like the beating of tribal drums, the outer, shifting circle of female figures urging them on.

"La, la."

The hysteria of the women's screams wove together with the

rhythm of Bertha's hands upon his head.

When the circles broke apart, the neighbors slipping silently through the twilight to their homes, Danny darted out to look at what they left behind. Nathan's memory left him leaning still against Bertha's wide body, both of them mesmerized by the violence they had seen below.

Nathan ran now from the rustling in the weeds with the reflexes of one who has long expected terror. His mother's screams echoed in his ear.

He thought he had forgotten that story, forgotten all the times Danny used to scare him with it when they were little, repeating it to him as the crowning tale of all the true ghost stories they shared when their parents had turned off the lights and gone to bed. Nathan had forgotten the details, except for a vague fear of twilight figures circling, and of women's cries. Until the night he woke, sensing that Danny was missing before he peered over to his brother's bed. Danny was gone, Nathan could tell that much even before his groping fingers found his glasses on the night stand. But his mother was the first to know, and Nathan, tumbling after her down the stairs, heard her scream and scream when she opened the bathroom door, and into his half-asleep mind had come a picture of himself fixed to the porch while Danny ran out to see the battered body of a dead snake.

Nathan reached the shade of the trees. He stopped running. The sweat soaking his back began to dry and he was cool for the first time since he'd left camp. His breathing slowed.

There was just space enough between the trees and underbrush for him to squeeze through. Low branches swept against his ribs as he passed. He ducked under taller limbs; leaves tickled his head. Instinctively he dodged in and out seeking the clearest spots, as though following a trail. Here, his steps were muffled by wet-black rotting leaves which clung to his sneakers and revealed more years' worth of leaves which had pressed down into rich soil. He hopped up on a great log only to feel it crumble damply beneath his feet. This was a kind of twilight world, as alien to the briarpatch as underwater to the sky. Green pressed down on him; the smell of damp earth rose up. It was as though he had walked forward several hours into the sudden coolness of an early summer evening.

The land sloped gently downhill. Where a giant tree had tipped across a deep gully was a cave, formed by the thick roots and an outcropping of rock. A heavy spider web crossed and re-crossed the opening. Peering in, Nathan found a thin spring bubbling up beside the rock.

If you're hiking and get lost, Danny had counselled him years ago when he still belonged to the Boy Scouts, what you do is, walk downhill. If you can, follow a stream. It's bound to lead to something. A road or some sort of community. It's better to go on than to try and figure out which way you came from. Your mind will play all kinds of tricks on you and you'll end up walking around in circles.

"O.K., Danny," Nathan said, and walked downhill, cheered when he discovered the spring trickling in the damp leaves beside him in a weak stream. It was like a sign. He followed it, down, down, hearing now and again the faint call of a far-away bird. The forest changed again; rhododendrons opened around him in sudden pink flare. Everywhere he turned were the flat glossy leaves. He had to push the branches from his face in order to see; he was wading through rhododendron and he felt he could hardly breathe. It went on forever and he was trapped, cut off from sound, sunlight, time. He'd known better than to get himself lost. He'd grown up on the stories Danny read from the newspaper about the children of tourists who stepped away from their parents on a mountain trail for one moment of exploring and disappeared. Swallowed up by the forest. Somebody was always getting lost, in spite of all the official signs that warned hikers to stick to the marked trails. Then the family and the park rangers and the sheriff and volunteers from all over the county would hunt night and day. A mammoth waste of human time, his father said, all because some rattle-brained mother couldn't keep track of her kids. It seemed like they rarely found lost children, even when they used helicopters and trained dogs. Bears, Danny told him. There's no way the kid could have starved to death so fast, and besides, where did his bones and stuff go to? You don't just vanish into thin air, unless something eats you.

You stay put if you ever get lost, his father said. Someone has a chance of finding you if you'll just stay put. You only make it worse if you keep walking. Nathan doubted that. Mom and Aunt Mae would be down at the lake until the sun went down. He didn't plan to stay out here that long. He would keep going. He took deep breaths to control his panic and forced himself to push on through the thicket.

And, like Danny said, the stream led him down to where the rhododendron thicket opened out onto a wide meadow, grass curling yellow and pale green. The stream cut a proud wide swath across its center. Nathan flung his arms up to a sky he could again see, and spun around in jubilant circles to watch clouds piled high rotate above him. Still spinning, he tripped over the first stone and fell. His outstretched arms took the weight of his upper body, saving him from smashing his head onto the other stones which lay about. Nathan rested on his elbows as he did in gym class when exhausted by push-ups, and scowled into the spikes of grass unfolding inches from his face. Each blade stood clear and separate from the others; he could see where each poked into the dirt beneath. The oblong stones were nearly hidden in the grass, which met over them. You had to catch a glint of gray within the green to know they were there. Or fall over them. Nathan propped his chin in his hands. The smooth-looking surface of the stone he'd missed was actually pitted; a crack ran across its center. The outlines of the stones beyond were blurred, as was the heap beyond them, and only by squinting hard did he identify the sudden shaft past that as the remains of a chimney that they must have tumbled from, and it had no outline at all but blended remorselessly into a blank background.

"Damn!" he said. "My glasses." The straight line of black beside his hand was, indeed, an earpiece. The lenses and other earpiece, still intact, were nearby.

"Now what am I going to do?" He sat up, squinting hard to bring the chaos around him into focus. He was sitting in a level square of grass free of bushes or brambles, oddly smooth except for the stones. Somebody's old cabin, he thought. Just my luck. I find a house and nobody's lived in it for a hundred years. He paced off the square, kicking at white bits of what turned out to be shards of china when he bent to examine them, the yellow-sprigged pieces of a teapot. He poked at them with a stick, wondering if he would stumble across something valuable buried here which he could take home. If he ever got home. He should have stayed put when he first realized he was lost. He shouldn't have left the campsite in the first place. It wouldn't have been that bad spending another day with his mom and LeeLee and Aunt Mae. Longing to be with his family the way they used to be rose up in his throat. No matter what they did to one another, to him, he was secure with them. He could count on them to behave with a certain consistency, could move among them without having to acknowledge his isolation, without having to feel much of anything. Being at home meant being in a kind of mindless way and there was comfort in that, as there was comfort in eating the same peanut butter on slightly stale bread for lunch every day. (Danny, opening his lunch sack on the way to school once and starting to eat his sandwich which was already somewhat mashed by the apple, baggie of carrots and two oreo cookies placed on top of it, had commented, I wonder why the bread is always stale? I mean, it had to have been fresh sometime.) You might not particularly like it, but you knew what to expect.

Nathan knelt to examine some rusty coils near the chimney. Springs from an iron bedstead. The cabin must have had only one room for eating and sleeping. He hoped it hadn't housed too large a family. He could picture them huddled here by the fireplace after the sun went down. The mother would be knitting in a chair closest to the light of the flames, the father dozing off in the other corner, and in between, a mess of kids pushing and squabbling among themselves for the warmest place. All the children would look like one another and like their parents, the way they did in those photographs of pioneer families in his history book at school. He used to pore over those pictures, fascinated by the rows and rows of barefoot children standing before the low cabins and glaring into the camera as though they were accusing him of something.

"You there. You. Boy. What are you doing on my land?"

It was a voice out of one of those yellowed photographs, and it startled him as the voice of his history teacher did when she broke in on his imaginings to ask him who the first governor of North Carolina was.

"Are you deaf, boy? What are you doing on my land?"

It was the scratchy-throated voice of an old woman, and she sounded mad. Nathan dropped the stick and peered at a wide dark mass among the taller shapes of trees. Nothing moved. There couldn't be anybody there. He was imagining things.

"Well?"

He held his glasses up to his eyes and a house sprang out of the vague bulk of shadow. It was not a house like he was used to seeing. Set well back in a clump of trees, your eyes could almost skim past and miss it. There was no real yard to mark its presence, just a mess of wild rose bushes and weeds. The walls were river rock, darker and more variously shaped than those he'd stumbled over beside the ruined cabin. Weeds wound up a low stone porch; ivy, creeping around the stone towards wide curtainless windows, seemed to grow right inside. The roof hung low over the walls, pulled down like the brim of a hat across a murderer's eyes. No one would live way out here. But on the porch a cane rocking chair still swayed gently. Then a figure stepped from the shadows. She must have been watching him this whole time. Nathan's hand dropped to his side, but the immediate blur so startled him that he quickly held his glasses in place again.

The old woman had come forward, her arms gripping the porch rail as though ready to swing her over for battle.

"I didn't know anyone lived around here," Nathan began. "I'm sorry if I scared you."

"Scared me?" She moved back into the shadow, snorting. "Looks like you're the one scared."

Nathan ducked his head in shame. But he wasn't about to tell her that what frightened him more than anything she might do or say had been his inability, when he first heard her voice, to decide whether or not she was real. That more than anything else, he was afraid of losing touch with reality like they said Danny had.

"Well, come up on the porch so I can get a look at you."

Nathan picked his way over to the house. Instead of steps, a long stone had been laid close to the house. He clambered up, into the comparative chill of the ivy-shaded porch. They stared at one another, each waiting for the other to speak. Her ponytail of straight light hair was like LeeLee's. But this woman didn't bother with ribbons, nor with a comb, much. Her hair was slicked back into a rubber band with the part all crooked like she didn't use a mirror, either. The arms below the rolled-up man's shirt sleeves were brown, the muscles stringy with age. She squinted unblinkingly at him with eyes like those of some fierce bird.

"I'm lost," he admitted. "I haven't seen anybody all day."

Her laugh shot straight from her throat, a cracked dry sound full of delight. "I haven't seen anybody all month. I wasn't planning to see anyone till I went into town next week for some groceries. But as long as you're here, you might as well come inside."

She disappeared through a screen door. Before it slammed shut, she tipped her head through and called back, "I have plenty of cold mint water. Also lemonade. You can take your choice."

"Lemonade, please." He followed the old woman inside.

"It's not as crazy as you think, an old woman living out here all alone. Some people do best in solitude, and I've come to understand that I am one of them."

She informed Nathan of this while he bathed his face and arms in her deep kitchen sink. Then she made him wipe his skin with cotton puffs soaked in witch hazel. "If you've been tramping around the woods as long as you say you have, you're probably covered with bug bites and poison ivy. There's no use encouraging them to itch, unless you enjoy misery."

She directed him around the low bookshelves which separated the room into two parts. He sat tentatively in a rocking chair, trying to keep it still. The shelves were heavy with musty dark-spined novels; set along the top, pottery bowls filled with stones and nuts and bits of china like the shards he had found outside. The woman cleared a space for a tray of glasses and sandwiches, then settled herself across from him in a cane-bottomed rocker, rocking it in a comfortable silence as though they were two old people before a winter fire. All the chairs on this side of the room were rockers, Nathan saw, grouped for conversation at either end of the room around two fireplaces now cold for summer. In each hearth stood stone milk jugs holding dried grasses.

She took a slow sip from her glass as though tasting lemonade for the first time and gauging whether or not she approved. She must have liked it, for she tasted it again, touching the tip of her tongue to her upper lip after each sip like a child after chocolate.

"I don't know your name," Nathan said at last.

"No." She set her empty glass on the floor and folded her hands carefully in her lap. "It's Hannah Louise, if you need to know. I'm named after my grandmothers."

"But what's your last name?" he asked politely.

"I'm not young enough to be at that sticky age where it bothers me to have you call me by my given name." She grinned at his confusion, rocking steadily for some moments. "I had two grandmothers," she said. "Both dead now, of course."

"I'm sorry." He said it automatically. It was the sort of thing his mother would have said.

"It's all right. Things die." She said it grandly, as though announcing a discovery. "I'm as old now as my grandmothers were when I was young. It's hard to believe. I don't feel that old, really. Most of the time I catch myself thinking the way I always have, the way I thought when I was young, a little girl. I want to run after butterflies, and eat whole batches of fresh cookies. Maybe I should ask somebody if this is the way I should feel. But there's no one old enough to ask. Just me." She bent forward, her voice low and confiding. "My grandmother Louise used to beat my daddy black and blue. She didn't kill him, but I think she wanted to." She leaned back in her rocker. "I never saw that, of course. That was when she was middle-aged and Daddy was a little boy. But every time Daddy whipped us, he would tell us how hard she hit him. Maybe he thought it would make us feel better. Does your father whip you?"

"Oh, no. He would never do anything like that. I don't think he's ever spanked any of us." Not even Danny. Nathan's arm ached from holding his glasses up to his eyes, but he was afraid to relax it.

"Well, now, you've been lucky. Or maybe you are just exceptionally well-behaved." She gave a chortle of laughter. Nathan smiled weakly back. "Though there are many ways of punishing people. My mama, for instance, she was always feeling what she called faint. No doctor can disagree with that diagnosis; there's nothing specific enough about it to label true or false. Mama treated herself. She lay in bed in the back room all afternoon and took medicine. We weren't to disturb her, no matter what. Not even when Austin broke his arm; we went down the road to the neighbors. But Austin and me—my little brother, Austin—we would sneak into her room and watch her nap. I've never known anybody sleep so much. Until I got older, I thought that's what women were supposed to do all day. Once we drank some of her medicine, right as she was lying there asleep. It came in a brown bottle. It tasted awful." She wrinkled her nose, and for a flash of time, Nathan could see a little girl peering out at him as if around a corner of a door, teasing, mischievous, egging on or maybe egged on by the someone beside her. Then he realized that she was staring back at him.

"Now you're staring," she accused. "Where are those manners?"

"I'm sorry," he said again, helplessly. The way she leapt from past to present was confusing him, or maybe he was the one who was doing the leaping. It worried him, that he couldn't seem to stay on one track, that Hannah Louise seemed at once old woman and little girl. He leaned to one side to rest his arm on the chair. He had to keep his vision straight.

"You broke your glasses." Hannah Louise's voice was suddenly brisk. "Give them to me and I'll fix them."

It was with great reluctance that he laid them in her dry palm. Would she, as that little girl would have done, grab them and run, taunting him over her shoulder? She started to rise, and he coiled to spring after her, knock her down if he had to, get his glasses back. But she was still straightening her knees, clinging to one arm of the rocking chair while she, slowly, uncurled her back and stood. It was a long process. He moved involuntarily to help her, and she shot him a quick look. "Do you think I sit around up here waiting for assistance? I'm old, young man, but I'm not helpless. Nor am I," and she, balance recovered, stepped briskly into the kitchen and right to a small drawer from which she removed tape, thin surgical-looking scissors, a bit of wire, "feeble-minded."

He didn't offer help again, but watched while she deftly pieced his glasses together. "I was the fixer in our family," she said as she worked. "I could fix things that Daddy would give up on and want to throw out. The sewing machine. Our old clock. Austin's bicycle. Austin always came to me when he had a flat tire. And I've been living up here alone for so long that whatever I didn't know then I've had to learn."

Curiosity pulled the question from him, despite his mother's warning: never, never ask a personal question, pick up what you can from what a person volunteers. "Didn't you ever get married?"

She laughed at him. "Women don't always, you know." She smiled then. "Yes, I was married for a while. My husband was an Indian. I met him when I went to Cherokee to teach at the school." She was busy with the tape for a few moments, wrapping it carefully around the earpiece. "We were married for three years, and then there was an accident on the construction site where he worked. He had been working so hard, trying to get money for our own land."

"And you bought it," Nathan prompted. "You came up here."

"I had to," she said simply. "We had agreed it was what we needed to do above everything else. He needed to own good land, after the reservation. That's all that mattered, getting a place of our own."

"It's strange." Nathan hesitated, sensing a new kind of power. For the first time in his life he felt able to shape his thoughts into words that would express them exactly. It had something to do, he thought, with Hannah talking to him so directly, not tiptoeing around the awkward parts of her story because he was too young, or because, as his mother was always saying, people shouldn't talk about such things. Words began to flow from him, effortlessly as blood from a wound. "I mean, it's strange that when you yelled at me outside I got a picture in my head before I even saw you of this pioneer woman standing in front of a cabin not much taller than she was. She had on a sunbonnet and a long shapeless dress and she held a rifle in two hands like it was a broom. There was a whole bunch of kids around her, all of them glaring into the camera like it was some sort of trespasser. You could tell from their faces that they'd had a hard time hanging onto their home, their land. But they also, every one of them, looked proud, like they'd go through it all again." Embarrassed at having spoken his vision so clearly, Nathan stumbled to a halt. "Anyway, that's what you are. I mean," he corrected himself, "you're not withered up and grim-looking like that woman was—"

"At least, I'm not carrying a rifle," Hannah put in, grinning.

He flushed, but had to finish. "But you are a kind of pioneer. You live off by yourself with only yourself to depend on. You came here because you had an ideal of something you had to do. Just like the early settlers in the mountains, walking up here miles and miles to find freedom."

"No, to find land. Freedom comes later, if it comes. Though there's not much liberty being a farmer, dependent on the soil and the seasons. But you do know that nobody can come onto your land and interfere with you without your permission."

"I wandered right onto your property without asking."

Hannah smiled. "I knew you were there. And I stopped you, didn't I, from exploring any more before I found out who you were and why you were out there."

"You still don't know who I am," Nathan pointed out, but a little doubtfully.

"Your name and address, no. But I know things about you that are more important."

"Such as?" he challenged.

"Now don't tell me that you've never met someone and felt right away that the two of you shared something, that in some special way you might not have even dreamed about the two of you are connected."

"No." It made Nathan lonelier than ever to realize how little he understood this lady. Once again, he felt, for no good reason, homesick.

Hannah spoke gently. "No. Perhaps you haven't felt it yet. Or allowed yourself to recognize what it was you felt. Here, I'll tell you what I know about you, and you'll see I didn't mean to trouble you." While she studied him, Nathan had an odd sense that she was calculating how much she should tell him, rather than how much she could. "Well," she began, "you're not afraid to ask about things, and you're polite enough to listen when someone tells you about them. You're a good listener. In fact, you're too good. I think you're cautious when you're with people, as if you're afraid you're going to give a part of yourself away. As if you've settled in your mind before you're"—and she cast a quick look over him—"before you're thirteen that people aren't to be trusted. That's too bad, because you're only going to get better at building walls as you grow older.

"Am I right?"

Nathan shrugged. "I'll be thirteen in December."

She clapped her hands. "Do you see what I mean? You won't trust me with a thing! Yes, I am quite right about you." In her delight, she smiled across the counter at him like a child who beats a grown-up in a guessing game. Nathan felt his earlier lonely feeling slipping away.

"My name is Nathan," he offered. "I live in Asheville with my mom and my sister LeeLee. And for now, with my Aunt Mae. She came down from Boston to help take care of us when my dad left."

"Ran out on you, did he?" She was polishing the lenses of his glasses with a soft rag.

"No!" Nathan said. "It wasn't like that at all." He closed his eyes for a moment, to try to explain how it was, but all he could see was his father's apartment that first weekend Nathan took the bus to Greensboro. The rooms were so empty and quiet. Nathan had come out of the bathroom in the middle of the night and there was Daniel sitting in the living room watching television with the sound turned down so low you could hardly hear it. His father never watched television; he used to be furious if he came home early from the university and they were lying in front of re-runs of "Gilligan's Island." "You boys need to be outside," he'd say, and switch off the set. Before he'd even said hello or put down his briefcase. But there he was, sort of slumped back in his chair with his feet spread apart on the coffee table (he had never allowed them to put their feet on the furniture!) looking like an old man, looking lost. It made Nathan uneasy to see him staring at Johnny Carson as if he were his only companion. It was like the way the apartment refrigerator didn't have anything in it but a tiny carton of skim milk and three eggs; none of the leftovers in plastic bowls, the half-empty jars of mustard and pickles and four different kinds of jam which filled the refrigerator at home. Nathan felt that he should do something to make his father look less lonely. Sit on the couch and watch Johnny Carson with him. Tell him about school. There was a guy in soccer who still hugged his dad sometimes; Nathan had seen them together after games.

But he hadn't been able to reach out. There was too much between them. He had just walked back down the hall to the study where he had spread his sleeping bag, and pretended that he hadn't noticed anything.

"Well, how was it, then?" Hannah handed him his glasses. When he put them on, the room sprang into focus, everything brighter than it had been, and slightly tilted. Hannah held her head tipped to one side as she waited for his answer; it wasn't just that the earpiece was crooked.

"My father's not an irresponsible man," Nathan told her, though as he spoke he could hear his mother's voice on the day after the funeral when Daniel had simply walked down the stairs with two suitcases and gone back for his typewriter and books without

saying anything more than "I'm leaving, Justina." His mother had
said plenty more, bolting up the stairs after him, dropping a pile
of towels and a string of furious protestations behind her. "Damn
you, Daniel, you've got to take some responsibility for this," was
the last one Nathan heard before he slammed the basement door
on them.

"It's just that my family—" he began. He hadn't thought of them
as a family, this past year, but at the word, he felt that their lives—
his and those of the people who surrounded him and shaped his
moments even when he was not with them—had begun to assume
a kind of order. He had been so afraid, after the funeral, that they
would move too quickly into new habits which would scarcely
acknowledge that there had been a disruption in their lives. That
they wouldn't, after all, make a life of grief, but would go along as
though the hole in the family had been patched up.

Hannah was a good listener. Her brown eyes rested steadily on
him, and he felt her draw his words into herself so that what he said
took on substance. He thought he could tell her all about Danny
and she wouldn't mind. Was this the feeling she had described
to him, this sense of being completely at ease with someone you
didn't really know? Was it because she was, deep down, like him?
Or, and he couldn't quite straighten out his thought, but left it as
an impulse vaguely shaped, was it that she was like someone that
he ought to know but didn't?

She didn't fiddle with anything in the kitchen once she'd put
away the tape and scissors, but gave him her full attention, never
taking her eyes from his. So that as he spoke, he felt everything
which had seemed haphazard and makeshift, uncared for in their
lives, begin to take on a pattern. It began to seem all right that his
mother worked and wasn't home until time to sit down for the
supper Aunt Mae prepared before she drove off to play music at
the restaurant up at the resort, that he and LeeLee had to whisper
in the mornings so they wouldn't wake their aunt up, that Nathan
visited his father only once a month.

Nathan saw the table set for the three of them, Mom, LeeLee
and himself, and Aunt Mae leaning against the stove to eat a bite of
whatever she had cooked before she had to leave for work. She ate
quickly, spooning her supper from a soup bowl, then lit a cigarette.

No matter how late it was that she was going to be out, and on weekend nights it was very late indeed, she always stood there, flicking ashes into the empty bowl (winking at LeeLee when she did, because they knew what Mom would say about that habit) and listened to LeeLee talk. Last week LeeLee had been in tears about a card that the country club clique was passing around which ranked the girls in their class in order of looks. LeeLee was near the bottom or maybe on the bottom; Nathan would have put her there himself, if asked. Aunt Mae listened, watching out of eyes that were dark like Danny's, sipping coffee from the mug Danny had made for her. "I'm not going to tell you that this will help any," she told LeeLee. "But when I was your age, I was so ugly that my own father wouldn't have denied it. I was skinny as a lamp post, and taller than your mama even then, and I had to wear her handed-down skirts and let me tell you, they were short. I looked like a farm girl fresh off the truck. There was nothing to do but pretend I didn't notice the difference between the way I looked and the way other girls did. About all you can do, sweetie, is ignore them. My mother told me that if girls felt better about themselves they wouldn't have to pick on each other so much. That a lot of them just go through a mean stage." She stubbed out her cigarette. "Though I'm not sure they all grow out of that."

Then she'd asked, "Does that help?" When LeeLee nodded, Aunt Mae had pulled her over in a quick, one-armed hug. "You're lying. There's not a thing in the world I can say that's going to make growing up any easier for you. You're going to have to go through it on your own. Maybe the things I can tell you will fit, some of them. But still that's just me talking. You're going to have to develop your own inside voice to tell you what to do, your own kind of guardian angel."

"Your aunt sounds like a pretty special person. You must be glad she's staying with you," Hannah said.

"I guess."

Nathan frowned, remembering that Aunt Mae had glanced over LeeLee's head to the table where he sat drinking a glass of milk, looking like she had wanted to say something to him, too. He'd gotten out of there fast, leaving his empty glass on the table— despite his mother's rule about putting dirty dishes in the sink. Let his sister listen to a bunch of advice; his policy was to ignore his aunt as much as possible. She'd come down for the funeral, and, without anyone inviting her, had just stayed on. If it weren't for her, he was sure his dad wouldn't have accepted the job in Greensboro and moved out. If it hadn't been for her, his mother would never have gone out on her own and gotten a job. A mother's place is with her children, she'd always said. She should be at home in case they need her. Not that mine ever have, mom always added; they're a fine, independent set of kids. Aunt Mae had even taken over the room he used to share with Danny. Because it was the largest and had a good view of the mountains, his mother explained, but to Nathan it was just one more sign of his aunt disrupting their lives. With her in the house he had to face every day that his dad had his own apartment, that his mother enjoyed getting away from home, that it didn't matter if he had a room big enough to share because when vacation came around, Danny wouldn't be coming home.

Hannah was looking at him expectantly.

"It was o.k. when Aunt Mae visited us," he said slowly. "She always had lots to tell us about living in Boston. She would bring us things from the art museums. She kept inviting us to come stay with her and go see the historic stuff. But having her move in—" He found himself unable to explain his resentment to Hannah. "Everything's different," he ended.

"Things are always changing." Hannah stretched to look out her kitchen window. "One thing, Nathan, if you live in a world of facts, you can't deny them."

Nathan shrugged, refused to look at her.

"Did you ever stop to think that your Aunt Mae might prefer to get back to living her own life?"

Why doesn't she then? was his immediate reply, but he couldn't say that out loud. "I guess I never thought about it," he found himself admitting. "I know she's got some guy up in Boston who's always sending her letters. Another musician, I think. I've heard her talk about him to Mom."

"There you are then," Hannah nodded her approval.

"Where am I, then?" he asked, almost rudely.

"Don't you expect that your aunt will leave you as soon as things have settled down a bit?"

What things? he wanted to shout back at her. What do you know about my family? Why should anything ever settle down again? Aunt Mae's stirred everything up; Danny stirred everything up. Danny ruined everything. But Hannah didn't say anything else so he couldn't shout at her.

He could hear a fly buzz against the window screen. As usual, putting his glasses on seemed to sharpen all his senses. Without them, he not only felt that he was walking in the dark, but that his hearing shut down, too, so that he was encased in a dark tunnel whose walls gradually seemed to shrink in upon him. He fought the impulse, now, to pull his glasses off and curl up in that grey, quiet world.

Hannah touched his arm. "Right now, I expect your body is telling you that you need a rest after so much time in the sun. Come on, I'll show you to a room where you can lie down for a few minutes."

Along the short hallway from the kitchen dozens of black and white photographs formed a line broken only by closed doors. There were family pictures: groups of children in white dresses kneeling beside their parents' wicker chairs; fat-cheeked babies gripping strings of beads; several of a little girl with thin curly hair and wistful eyes. There was, further along, an autographed photograph of Eleanor Roosevelt and then some hand-tinted prints of the mountains. Hannah opened the door to a small room which had strings of dried beans looped from window to window like crepe paper at a party. It was furnished simply, an iron bedstead, a narrow rolltop desk with the top rolled down, more dark-spined novels in a glass-doored cabinet.

She fluffed a pillow on the bed. "I'll wake you in an hour if you're not already up. If you sleep too long in this heat you'll be groggy the rest of the day." She paused in the doorway. "I'll be in the garden out back if you need anything."

Nathan stretched out on the quilt, first placing his sneakers side by side on the rag rug. He couldn't sleep at first, uneasy at the thought that Hannah might be nearby, might be listening for him. But the door was closed; she'd closed it herself. She said she was going outside. What was wrong with him, that he was so eager to suspect that there was something strange about this? He'd never spent any time with anybody who was, well, loony; why did he think he knew so much about it? You guys are crazy; LeeLee used to look at the two of them with a pained expression while their laughter came leaking out, despite their efforts to squeeze it back. Danny could be so funny! If the house was burning down and it's a choice between us and the old man's book, he'd say, and then pause for effect, well, I'd get ready to jump out the second floor window if I were you. He cracked Nathan up. LeeLee just frowned at them, her opinion perfectly clear from her expression.

You could tell if someone was crazy. There didn't have to be obvious signs, a continual twitching of the head, an outspoken belief in the existence of little men in the closet. You could sense it in the way they talked. His father used to look funny whenever Nathan mentioned Mr. Taylor down the street who shot squirrels off the telephone lines. But he never said anything about him outright. Was Mr. Taylor crazy?

At least Hannah Louise wasn't hurting anybody. But what about him? Did other people feel around him the way he felt around Hannah, that he was different? At school they had treated him so delicately ever since Thanksgiving. Even the other kids seemed to pick and choose what they said to him. He could tell his teachers were thinking all kinds of things they would never say out loud about his family. They made him feel sorry for himself. He dreaded going into classes; once there, he tried to stay as inconspicuous as possible. Except for biology. He could breathe in there. Mrs. Greene didn't go easy on anybody. Dead or dying, she'd expect you to sit up straight and have your homework done. She'd graded him down for every day his biology notebook was late the time he left it at his father's place in Greensboro. But there must be something about him that alerted people that he was a crazy kid from a crazy family, that he was just like Danny and would end up doing what Danny had done and there was nothing he could do to stop it. Blood trickled across gleaming white tile; Nathan shuddered and closed his eyes, resolved to sleep and forget about them all.

He couldn't, of course. His mind kept tossing back and forth: crazy, or not? Surely if he was lying here able to figure out reasons why he wasn't, surely that was proof of sanity. That he could do what he had to do. But then Danny had always kept a level head. He'd yelled back at the folks, but that ought to be expected, the way they used to pick at him and at each other. Nathan felt like beating his fists into the mattress. Why hadn't they told him what was wrong with Danny? Why did he have to be haunted by not knowing? Why couldn't Danny have told him anything? On TV, people who killed themselves left notes. If Danny had left a note, they hadn't shown it to him. One more little detail hushed up. Nathan rolled onto his other side. Hush up enough of the details and you can pretend that nothing happened. Or at least, that whatever happened doesn't affect you. That was their philosophy. Tell everybody that Danny died in a car wreck, and pretty soon, you can believe it yourself. Nathan grinned; now *that* was crazy. It had gotten to the point that he didn't know what had really happened to Danny. He was afraid to talk to anybody about it, for fear of telling the truth to someone who wasn't supposed to know it. And so, because he knew that he was lying, and because he knew that his parents were lying, and because he couldn't be sure who else was lying when they told him how sorry they were that his brother had been in a car accident, he couldn't trust anybody.

When the funeral was over, he'd had to get away by himself, get away from the confusion of not knowing who knew what, not knowing who to ask about Danny. He'd gone down to the basement and called Jed in out of the rain. The living room upstairs undulated with heads nodding to one another, playing the game, bending forward for food, bobbing up to drink, leaning down to speak and popping up again. The neighbor women were in and out of the kitchen. They'd come early that morning to fix coffee and make biscuits, and now urged people to eat, and just as urgently gathered up dirty plates to wash. Even with the door closed he could hear the roar of conversation. It sounded like a party up there. Which his mother ruled, sitting in the middle of the crowd in her gold-embroidered arm chair, looking limp and beautiful as she accepted condolences, giving nothing away.

The basement door had opened and the voices upstairs resolved themselves into individual strands. His father; Mrs. Reuben from next door offering coffee; a cousin, laughing.

"Well, Robert Combs, after all these years," he heard Aunt Mae say. "Justina's in the living room. I'm sure she'll be glad to see you. Go speak to her." Then the door closed and the voices blurred again.

His aunt lowered herself to the step above him, smoothing her grey skirt over her knees. "I thought you might be down here," she said. "Where's LeeLee?"

"Probably in her room with a book." Nathan continued to scratch at the base of Jed's ears, digging in a little with his fingers so the dog squirmed in delight.

"That's one contented-looking dog."

"It's okay for him to be inside as long as he stays downstairs." His voice had been defiant.

"I wouldn't want to be outside in this weather, either." Aunt Mae leaned her chin on her knees. "I always hated November."

Nathan cradled Jed's head between his hands. "He's really Danny's dog," he said. "I started taking care of him when Danny went away to school. Danny was going to trade me something for doing it, but I didn't want anything. It was nice to have a dog that was just like my own."

"He'll miss Danny, too," Aunt Mae said. "He won't understand why he doesn't come back."

"Dogs aren't dumb," Nathan said. "I told him what happened. What really happened," he added, without looking at his aunt.

Aunt Mae stretched out her hand and touched Jed's back. "Danny needed something from us that he didn't get. We weren't responsive in the right way, weren't responsible. Though I don't know if he knew himself exactly what he did need. He was confused. The signals between all of us were confused."

"But he wasn't crazy," Nathan said fiercely. "Dad said—." He stopped. "Danny was never crazy."

He felt her looking at him intently, like she was getting ready to say something. But before she could, the door above them had opened. There was a sudden flow of warm air and kitchen noises. "Who let that dog in here?" Justina asked.

"He's just in the basement," Nathan said.

"It's pouring rain out," Aunt Mae said.

"You think I have the energy today to clean up whatever that dog tracks in? With all these people here and more coming all the time? Put him outside, right this minute."

Nathan walked to the door, snapping his fingers at Jed. "Come on, boy." Rain soaked through his sweater as he held the storm door open, pulling on Jed's collar, and nudging him with his knee to get him outside. Then Nathan had pushed past Aunt Mae and run upstairs, not bothering to close the kitchen door behind him.

"You certainly make a habit of stirring up my children." His mother's voice was icy. "I'd have thought you'd leave the rest of them alone."

"Nathan and I were talking about Danny." Aunt Mae's reply was so low he almost missed it. "You can't be jealous of that, today of all days. He needs to talk about his brother, about what happened, and the two of you are so caught up in your own warfare that you haven't even noticed him. And then this charade of telling everybody that Danny was killed in a car crash. What good is it to try to hide things? Isn't that what led to this in the first place? Pretending everything was all right with you, that you had a model family. You're only making things worse, Justina."

"Why, Nathan, there you are. Won't you have some of this delicious pound cake?" Mrs. Reuben from next door turned from the sink, wiping her hands on the dish towel which hung from her apron pocket. "You boys are always hungry, I know. There's no excuse for not eating, with all the fine food people are bringing in. Let me cut you a piece of cake with a glass of milk."

He had moved guiltily away from the door, leaving behind the furious rush of his mother's reply. "No, thank you, Mrs. Reuben," he said politely, and left the kitchen before she offered him something else.

He hadn't heard any more of what the two women said. He had spent the rest of the afternoon in his room, and missed the moment when Aunt Mae told his parents that she was going to stay with them for a while and why. That must have been a real showdown, Nathan thought, and for the first time in a long time he really felt like laughing. He could just picture the three of them in the living room; Daniel and Justina suddenly drawn together in self-defense against his aunt who would let nothing stop her from telling them that she didn't think they were tuned in to their own children's needs. He could just imagine his mother's face when her

childless and unmarried younger sister informed her that she knew
more about what her niece and nephew needed than their parents
did. "Now, Justina." He could hear Aunt Mae's voice, low and with
that lilt to it which to him had always seemed a consequence of
her profession when maybe after all it was one of the things which
made her herself, and made her the only one, that day, to attempt
to be honest with him.

But what business was it of hers, anyway? She wasn't really part
of the family. She had no right to interfere. She'd followed him
up to his room after one week in the house and waited in the
doorway until he'd had to look up from his homework. "Why
aren't you nicer to LeeLee?" she'd asked. "She's your sister." Just
remembering that made him mad all over again. The bedroom was
cool, but, caught in resentment, Nathan felt hotter than he had all
day. Irritation boiled up within him till his skin felt flushed with
fever. He turned the pillow over and over searching for a cool spot.

"LeeLee's dumb," was all he'd thought of to say to his aunt.
And "I have to finish my geography," said pointedly. She'd left him
alone then. Not that he could concentrate after that interruption.
What did it matter to his aunt how he got along with his sister?
They got along fine if they kept out of each other's way. They had
nothing in common. Though his mother liked to boast, when the
Cavins were around, that they looked like twins. As though it were
to her credit that both of them were short and fair-haired in a
family inclined to be taller than average and dark. LeeLee's hair was
wispy around her forehead, almost curly, and pulled into a long
braid in back, while Nathan's was cut straight across and usually
bleached almost to white by the time May came around because
he spent so much time outside. They'd been good friends until
they were seven and eight. He had played happily with LeeLee's
doll family, building houses and forts beneath the basement steps
where she kept them, acting out together stories she had read. In
turn, she followed him outside to explore the creek which ran
behind the house. They caught crawdads, making homes for them
in glass jars and trying to figure out what they would eat, before
turning them loose at supper time so they could crawl back to their
families. LeeLee had insisted on that. They also trapped tadpoles
and lightning bugs and yellow jackets—those by inverting a jar

over the clover where the bee was, then very quickly slipping the lid underneath. These last LeeLee agreed they should let suffocate, glad to be able to defeat one enemy of their summers. Because she trusted his knowledge of the outdoors, despite the fact that he couldn't yet read any of the descriptions in the plant and wildlife books he was given at birthdays, LeeLee ate whatever he pointed out as edible. He remembered two long afternoons spent training their puppy to hunt truffles, which he'd heard about on television. They were wild with delight when Jed began rooting hungrily in the earth beside the back patio, sure he understood at last that he was searching out treasures which would make their fortunes. Daniel had locked them both in their rooms for encouraging the dog to dig up his tulip bulbs.

All that time, Danny had wandered the neighborhood on his own, roaming with a gang of older boys, home only for meals and bedtime, showing no interest in what went on at home. Until one Saturday morning when he'd looked up from behind the cereal box at Nathan, who sat on the floor in front of the TV cutting a klee-nex box into a bed for LeeLee's youngest doll. Danny had stared at his brother while his spoon kept dipping into milk and dripping its way to his mouth and back to the bowl. When it finally came up empty, he spoke. "Aren't you a little old to be playing with that stuff?" was all he said, but that had been the end of it. After break-fast, Danny allowed him to tag along to a game of two-hand touch. When Nathan finally came home that afternoon, sweaty, muddy, one knee skinned and bruises on his ribs from being tackled by a heavier boy who forgot whenever it was convenient the rules of the football game, he didn't bother to ask his sister what she had done without him. Next day, she stood on the porch and watched them choose up teams for the football game. During a lull in the first half she came to the edge of the field—their front lawn—and he had shouted at her to go away and play with her dolls. The other boys didn't even notice her. She had turned away without answer-ing back, withdrew, he supposed, to the dark space beneath the steps where the doodle bugs rolled around and cobwebs from the steps brushed her head. After that he sometimes caught her staring at him over a book she held; once he was certain she was spying on them from her bedroom window; but she never asked him why he was ignoring her, and she never mentioned playing together.

Well, that had been a long time ago. You couldn't expect a little kid to be considerate of a girl's feelings. Anyway, it had been good for him to learn to play rough. If LeeLee wanted to play with them, all she had to do was ask. Girls in his class at school fought their way onto the soccer field now; they were really aggressive. Nobody stopped them from getting what they wanted. Some of them were pretty good, too. But LeeLee had let them push her around; she hadn't even tried. He and Danny had gotten in the habit of ignoring her completely.

And, so what? Except that Aunt Mae had tried to make him feel guilty about it. But it was none of her business how he treated his sister. She didn't know anything about him; she didn't know how things were. Aunt Mae just liked to stir up trouble.

"Though she wasn't like that as a girl." Justina had snapped a fresh pillowcase in the air before drawing it onto the pillow. She clenched the pillow in her teeth for the first bit, then gave a little grunt of effort as she pulled the case secure. Christmas holidays were over, their last, Nathan knew now, as a whole family. Danny and Aunt Mae had left for New England that morning, and Justina was changing every bed in the house. His offer to do his and Danny's curtly refused, Nathan sat crosslegged on the floor with a comic book, waiting for his mother to leave the room.

Justina plumped the pillow down on Danny's bed and turned to Nathan's. "She used to be the kind of girl who was always agreeable. It was hard to get her mad about anything. Like she made it her business to get along with people. Our grandmother said she was the kind of girl who would be a good wife. But she took it into her head that she had to study music, and then she wouldn't rest until she got up North to study at the conservatory." Justina tucked the top sheet at the foot of the mattress. "There's something that going North to school does to people. You can see the same thing happening to Danny since he started going up there. Losing respect, answering back."

"I thought you sent Danny away to school because he was running wild down here," Nathan ventured.

Justina turned on him. "Your father," she emphasized, "sent

Danny away to school because he thought Danny needed more of a challenge than he could get in the schools down here. Never mind that every one of the Cavins have gone to North Carolina public schools for generations. And turned out just fine, thank you. But that was his reason. Any change you see in your brother now you can blame on that school."

"Danny doesn't seem wild to me," Nathan mumbled.

"I suppose you didn't notice the way the two of them ganged up on your father at the dinner table. Ruining the Christmas dinner it took me hours to fix. You couldn't get a word in edgewise for the two of them. First Mae, then Danny."

Nathan was forced to abandon his position of neutrality. "They weren't criticizing Dad. Danny was just asking him questions about his work, about why he does what he does. That's all. It was just a discussion."

Justina jerked the spread up. "Your father couldn't finish his turkey for being attacked. Discussion we can do without at my dinner table, thank you." She had smoothed a final wrinkle and stalked from the room.

But they hadn't been attacking his father, Nathan thought. Danny had simply picked up on a question of Aunt Mae's which had gone around the table while the rice was being passed.

"Yes, why do you think history is so important, Dad? I mean, don't you think that what's happening to people today, right now, is important, too?"

Daniel, at the head of the table, with plenty of space between his chair and Nathan's and LeeLee's, took several bites of dressing which he chewed and swallowed before answering. "People who don't understand the past are condemned to repeat it."

"Yes, we all know that." Aunt Mae had broken the silence which followed, smiling at her brother-in-law. "Though you needn't make it sound so dismal. Surely there are pleasant pasts."

"Not around this house," Danny muttered.

"Excuse me?" Daniel looked across the table at his son. "The pleasant parts tend to be forgotten. It's the crises, the tragedies, that stick in the mind. Look at any newspaper; our minds tend to dwell on the disastrous side of things. Can't we have some hotter gravy, Justina?"

"How would you know what a newspaper says?" Danny burst out. "You haven't read one for years. We've taken the "Citizen-Times" and Sunday "Post" since before I can remember, and you don't look at either one."

"I'm sure Daniel reads when he can," Aunt Mae interrupted. "He has so many student papers to grade."

LeeLee, buttering bits of roll and just as steadily swallowing them down, said, "I thought his graduate assistant graded his papers for him."

Danny leaned forward on his elbows, his plate pushed to one side. "How can you honestly offer your students perspective on the past if you aren't keeping up with what's happening today?"

"Finish your dinner, Danny," Justina said.

"There's always TV," LeeLee offered.

"Or are you saying that everything worthwhile has already happened?" Danny let his question hang in the air. Aunt Mae turned expectantly to Daniel. Nathan quit twisting the fringes of the table-cloth into strands and knotted his fingers in his lap. He couldn't eat.

"I'm not saying anything. Damn it, Justina, aren't we going to have dessert?"

Really, Nathan thought, it hadn't been all that different from any other meal; there had just been more of a conversation going on, on top of the usual suppressed tensions. What had upset his mother, he had figured out, while looking at the bedroom door she had slammed shut, was that after cleaning up, Aunt Mae had disappeared with Danny and not come back until suppertime. "We're going on a walk," she had called up the basement steps, not inviting anyone else along. Justina had looked out after them, the little frown line flashing between her eyes. "You'd think he'd want to stay home with his family," she said.

"She's your sister." Daniel had waved a book at her. "You're the one who invited her for Christmas."

Nathan's bedroom door had flown open, for the second time, and Justina stepped back inside with a pile of blankets which she placed on Danny's bed. "It's good to get the house settled again," she said. "Everyone back where they belong. Having your aunt in the house, I feel like someone's always watching over my shoulder, second-guessing the way I do things."

Nathan lay flat on Hannah's bed, forcing his eyes open as wide as they would go. If he tried hard to stay awake, he would probably fall asleep. He knew what his mother had meant, that Christmas two years ago. Aunt Mae made him feel uneasy, too, like there was something she expected of him, something she expected him to give which he didn't know if he was ready to do. He didn't like feeling that way. But, and Nathan scowled at himself, he wasn't sure either if he liked seeing himself as somebody who just kept quiet all the time, kept out of the way, kept the peace.

He'd never talked to Aunt Mae about Danny. The closest he'd come was in the kitchen a few weeks ago. He'd just put a cheese sandwich under the broiler when she came in. He couldn't walk away and leave it to burn. Nor could he pull it out before the cheese at least started to melt; he didn't want to appear rude. He pretended that he hadn't noticed her, swiped with a sponge at the tomato seeds and juice puddled on the counter.

She was taking vegetables out of the refrigerator; that meant she'd be around for a while. He wouldn't be able to escape. Nathan had peered at his sandwich, willing the cheese to hurry up.

"I'm sorry I missed your big game last Saturday," she said. "I'd promised Jason I'd get to Boston for a concert. I had really hoped to see you play."

"It wasn't much," he muttered.

"I still remember walking with LeeLee to the field on the corner to watch you and Danny play soccer. The two of you were the whole team. The other guys just hung back and let you at it."

"That's not a great way to use a team," Nathan said. "We were lousy to be on a team with." The cheese had melted. He turned the broiler off and slid his sandwich onto a plate.

"Nathan." She spoke in a rush. "If you want to talk about it, I'm here."

"Right," he'd managed. "See you." He'd gotten out of there fast and up to his room where no one would see the grief which hit him. He left his plate untouched on the floor. They weren't supposed to eat upstairs, another of Daniel's rules (though, Danny had long ago pointed out, their father kept a special coffeemaker in his study and a tin of cookies). Well, good, he wasn't around to gripe about it. Why did Aunt Mae have to bug him with her memories, anyway? His mother was right; she just stirred people up.

"So why don't you leave us alone!" Nathan whispered loudly. The bedroom curtain flapped at the window as if in response. "We don't need you." His mother must have overheard Aunt Mae talking to him about Danny because at breakfast the next day she'd turned on him. "Are you crazy?" she'd asked. "What's gotten into you? You can't go flinging his life around like that. Have some consideration. If you want to talk about him, talk to me. I'm your mother. If you have to talk about him." She'd gotten up from the kitchen table and twitched the curtains over the sink so they hung exactly even, revealing her collection of little glass animals. The sun, striking these, spilled across the counter in violent reds and oranges and greens. "But I don't see why you need to talk about it. Christ, those endless discussions we used to have with that boy; school was wrong and we were wrong and he was wrong and everything was wrong. Why couldn't he pull himself together and get on with living? We all have to endure things we don't like. Nobody ever promised life would be easy. God knows mine hasn't been. I put my life on hold for seventeen years and nobody gave a damn. But there was always a wide streak of selfishness in Danny. You have to learn that the world doesn't revolve around you."

"I wasn't going to talk to her, Mom," he'd said, but his mother had rushed off to work without saying anything more.

"I didn't talk to her!" he whispered fiercely into his pillow, twisting his hands in the sheets. "I didn't say anything!" There was no reply but the soft flapping of cloth at the window, and Nathan tried to quiet the breath that seared his already aching throat.

Sometime later he curled more cozily into the patch of sun which warmed his back and made him unwilling to move though the bed was lumpy and he seemed to have lost his pillow for his head rested uncomfortably on his hands. Partially awake, he could control his dreams, could keep from slipping into nightmare. He could fantasize anything he liked, and he felt his mind slipping into a green meadow where a soft light glowed through the leaves and Marjorie Riddle grinned at him that peculiar one-sided grin as she tore pages from her biology notebook and scattered them across the grass. Nathan wanted to run to her, but there seemed to be something wrong with his breathing. It came in loud gasps; it would stifle him. But that wasn't his breathing. Nathan watched as his fantasy slid away from him as quietly as it had appeared. There weren't to be any good dreams. Next door, LeeLee tossed fretfully. And down the hall, his mother breathed in, paused as though she were listening, then breathed out again with a heavy sigh.

She didn't like for them to close their doors at night anymore. He got used to studying with his radio on for privacy. But when he put the light out, the noise of her breathing sometimes kept him awake for hours. The strident rhythm, in, out, seemed to force its pattern on him, to command that he breathe with her: in, out. He would take shorter and shorter breaths to break away; hers grew all the louder as his diminished until, indeed, her breathing almost stifled him. If he crept to his door and closed it, she would call out almost at once. "Nathan!" The slightest noise woke her now. This, too, oppressed him. On those sleepless nights he didn't dare reach for a book from the nightstand; her mattress would creak anxiously and she would cry, "Nathan. Is something wrong?"

He rolled over on his back and woke fully. The breathing had been, after all, his own, magnified by the stiff cotton of the starched sheets. He lay in the silence of a sultry afternoon, his neck stiff from sleeping without a pillow. Not quite in silence; there was a faint humming outside his window. Hannah Louise was tending her garden.

Hannah crouched in the dirt, balancing on her heels. From beneath a wide straw hat the long tail of her hair hung over her shoulder, brushing the ground as she worked. Her fingers molded soil around the base of a tomato plant. She tipped her head to one side long enough to call to Nathan, "Glad you're awake."

"Why?" He reached the last stepping stone laid at the garden's edge, then moved carefully around the weeded circle which bounded each plant, avoiding the faint depressions where their roots spread under the soil as he would respect the outline of an old gravemound.

"You are one for questions." Hannah rested her hands on her knees, bending her head to scratch her nose on her shirt collar. "Because. I always go swimming about this time of the afternoon and I thought you'd probably want to come along."

"All right!"

"I thought so." Pressing her hands on her knees, she pushed herself upright. She laid one hand on Nathan's shoulder and looked over her garden. "If I stand up too quickly, I get dizzy. A sure sign of old age."

"You're not that old."

"Old enough. I have to admit it. It's fact. The lake is through the trees on this side of the cove. Let's go."

She went first, breaking off branches which hung into the narrow trail. "Every time I come down this way I try to pull a few things out. Otherwise nature would take over this trail for good."

"It's got a pretty good start." Nathan slapped back a briar which hooked his arm.

"If you want a boulevard, go back to the Park. I understand they've marked the best spots for you to stand on when you want to get the most scenic pictures," she teased.

"It's not that bad. But it's not like this." The trail ended abruptly in a stand of river birch. The lake spread itself before him like a gift, clear olive green in the center, deep soft black along the banks where trees bent to touch their shadows. The wind murmuring through the rounded, rippling leaves made him want to dive right in and feel the water move against his skin.

"Of course, it's not all mine. I only own this corner. I don't know who the rest belongs to."

"You've never seen anyone around?" Nathan gazed enviously across to the woods on the far side.

"Never when I swim. Of course, there's always the possibility that somebody might, just might, come out of the woods over there. That gives skinnydipping some excitement."

Nathan grinned back at her. "I've never been skinnydipping."

"Well, I encourage you to try it some day." She had already unbuttoned her shirt and dropped her skirt to the ground with a graceful kick. Underneath she was wearing a faded swimsuit of a vague purple color. It hung loosely on her the way skin bags on the arms of older women. "In honor of a visitor," she explained.

Nathan knelt on the bank and stretched his arm down to the water. Already several feet deep at the shore, it remained shallow for some distance out and retained the heat of the sun. "It's like bathwater." He shook his arm dry, watching the droplets strike the surface.

"Not out in the middle. Or deep down. The sun only hits the top layers. It's icy once you stir it up some. There's a spring that feeds in."

A dragonfly dipped down, rested on the surface a moment before vibrating away. Smaller bugs floated, too tiny for Nathan to distinguish; he knew they were there by their reflections and the disturbance on the glass-green surface. Minnows flickered up, nibbling.

"I'm going in." Hannah thrust through the water until it covered

her waist, then turned and flopped over on her back. "Lovely," she
called, curling her head up to him like a turtle. She laid her face
back to the sky and pulled towards the middle of the lake with
a steady, sure backstroke. In the water, she could be any age; she
could be young.

"Aren't you coming in?" She treaded water, her head bobbing
like a buoy. When his family drove to Sugar Lake, used to drive,
his mother spent the afternoons lying on her lawnchair with the
straps and top of her swimsuit peeled down to get an even tan.
She would lie like that for hours, asleep for all they knew, except
that her dark glasses seemed to follow his every move the way the
blind eye of a submarine periscope turns continually after an alien
ship.

Nathan folded his clothes together and put them in the shade,
kicking his sneakers on top. He inspected his feet, disgusted at how
short and stubby they were. If you have big feet as a kid, Danny
told him, it's a sure sign you'll be tall. He'd never get as tall as
Danny. He didn't know why his mother bothered to save all those
clothes; he'd never grow into them. She had packed them away in
her closet once his dad moved his things out. "They'll fit someday,"
she assured him. He doubted it. But she'd keep them anyway.

"I've seen boys in their underwear before," Hannah yelled.
"Come on in."

He swam out to where she was floating on her back and then
beyond, to the shallows of the other side. If he had a canoe, he'd
tie it up here to a branch and sleep in the shade.

Floating is the best, Danny said. When you're on your back with
your ears underwater you can't hear anything but the kind of pulse
sound of your heart beating or the blood pulsing in your ears. You
can really focus in on how hard it beats, how long between each
beat. If you breathe real slow, you can make it beat slower and
slower. It must be as quiet as that just before you die.

They floated in the middle of the lake. The water was green
on Nathan's legs and feet. Wisps of clouds waited for him to float
beneath. When he moved closer to shore, he could calculate how
fast he was going by watching the approach of the tops of the pines.
Danny preferred to stay out in the middle.

You can't see anything but sky, Danny said. They sidestroked near each other so they could talk. If you keep watching it, after awhile even that starts to lose its color. You stare and stare and it's nothing but empty space and you feel like you could float right into it. But there's nothing there. You can't tell which way you're going. After awhile, you can't even tell if you're moving.

I get tired of floating way before that, Nathan said.

Sometimes I could just about fall asleep. If I didn't have to kick once in awhile to stay up, I would. Danny claimed he could float for a half hour at a time without moving his hands or feet. Nathan didn't believe this.

Your legs are too heavy. They'd sink, and you have to kick them back up or they'll pull you down.

No. Danny was stubborn. Watch me.

It was all coming together. As Nathan lay on the lake, his head gliding along the surface of the water, ears buried, just the right amount of face left a dry circle, it wasn't the old woman he glimpsed far down the line of his body, backstroking slowly towards the shore, but Danny, lying on his back beside the bathtub, head cradled in a blue towel, palms turned up, slightly cupped, open, relaxed as if awaiting a touch. He lay there so easily, floating, floating away, without feeling a thing.

Except for the pain. Nathan jerked over onto his stomach and began to swim hard for the shore. Streaks of blood on the tiles of the hall bathroom and slashes red on Danny's wrists. Vertical slashes, which followed the path of the vein. He pressed his face into the water, forcing himself to swim four and then eight strokes to a single breath, gasping, to rid himself of that pain and the sensing of it which made him sick. He had to feel his own arms reaching strong and whole, his hands attached and vigorous, thrusting into the water with no loose skin to flap open, gape open at the wrists. If he weren't swimming he would be sick, sick as he was on that night so that his mother had two boys to fret over, she complained later, though at the time she simply tripped over Nathan, who was being sick in the toilet, on her way to telephone an ambulance. Over the noise of his choking, he heard her cries fade down the stairs, and the noise of her wrenching the phone off the hook and dropping it to the floor.

And LeeLee, where had she been? Probably in her room with

a book, where she always was. Nathan had traced over the plot of
that night as he used to trace the lines in his arm where it lay on his
desk at school, studying, because there seemed nothing else worth
studying, the pathway of his veins running blue back to his heart.
They ran underground at his elbow; funny how there were parts
of yourself you never really saw. The cap of your elbow. Your nose,
though by closing one eye you could get a kind of fuzzy pink shape
that was the side of it. You can't see your nose, Danny insisted. Not
the thing in the mirror, that's just its reflection and backwards at
that. You can't see your own face, for that matter. You'll never really
know what you look like, don't you understand? All you'll know
about yourself is whatever other people tell you. And how can you
believe them?

Danny's face had changed before he went back to school in
the fall. LeeLee noticed it first. She started to tease him about getting wrinkles and Mom shut her up by making her clear the table.
We don't talk about people's appearance, she had admonished. It
wasn't wrinkles which made Danny different, but Nathan knew
what LeeLee was trying to say. Danny seemed suddenly older, de-
feated somehow. The skin was stretched across his cheekbones as
if it might tear if it were pulled any tighter. His mouth, which used
to be so generous-looking, always open to laugh or argue about
something, his mouth last fall had a pinched look, as though Danny
were shutting his lips hard against words he didn't want to come
out.

And I never asked you what was wrong. I just watched and
wondered. I thought your mouth was set against me, your brother.
I didn't know why. The rest of you was the same. Deepset dark
eyes that intensified to black when you concentrated. Brown hair
curling over your collar. Dad crabbed at you to get it cut, ordering
you around like you were just a kid, and you never answered back.
You didn't even tease LeeLee. Your face was a stone wall that let
nothing through.

Nathan struck at the water. If Hannah was watching him, let
her think he swam the way little kids do, all splash and wasted
energy. So what. Danny had been the one who made sure he knew
how to swim properly from the beginning. He'd had lessons like
any kid, of course. But he had been timid about getting far from

shore; without his glasses, he couldn't see the edge of the water, and worried about losing track of his direction. Danny had coaxed him out, had stayed with him. And Danny had left him without an explanation.

When they drove him to the Greensboro train station last fall, the rest of them acted like it was just another family outing, like there had been nothing different about the previous months. Daniel strode way ahead with the tickets, the others following up the long ramp to the platform carrying Danny's things. Danny had his suitcase; Mom walked beside him, arms folded around his good suit coat which she patted from time to time, brushing away, with anxious hands, invisible dust. Balanced on top she carried a paper sack of apples and peanut butter sandwiches, the ritual traveller's lunch. LeeLee wandered along behind, stopping to read timetables and old posters which advertised musicals in a long-closed down-town theater. She disappeared for a time behind a mass of children demanding orange slices from their mother. The tart smell of the juice made Nathan queasy in the overheated station. He walked behind Danny, head down, trying not to speculate about what had caused the brown stains on the dirty marble floor. If he hadn't been carrying Danny's knapsack slung over his shoulder he would have gone back to wait in the car. Only two trains a day came through this station; to Nathan, it seemed as hopeless as everything else that day.

On the platform the others huddled in gray overcoats against a sudden autumn rain, looking as dreary as a refugee family waiting to cross the border. One side of the station clock above them read one and one-half hours slow, Daniel pointed out several times. Nathan had a peculiar sense that they had missed that time: but where had they been then? And where would they be when the clock caught up with the time that it was now?

His parents filled the minutes with commentary. "It's the fourth time we've brought Danny to the station," said Daniel. "We drove him to Connecticut the first time, when he started school."

"But think of all those trips we took to Chicago to see your aunts," put in Justina. "Every time, the train was late."

"The train is always late. That's one of the pleasures of riding it." Daniel waved at the empty track. "You just have to sit back and relax and remember that there's not a thing you can do about getting there any faster. Learning to ride the train is an excellent exercise in self-control. The trouble with most people these days is that they're so filled with their own importance that they think that every minute of their day has to be filled with accomplishing something. People need to learn that there are things more important than they are."

"Like what?" LeeLee demanded, for once attending to a conversation. Justina moved off down the platform.

"Oh," Daniel looked vaguely at the sky. "Time. Trains."

"Education," Justina said firmly, returning. "Danny, you know how important these first weeks are. Did you pack your good shirt so it wouldn't wrinkle? The dean is sure to have some sort of reception for the seniors. I wish you'd let me pack for you."

"I don't understand," Daniel mused, "why it is that Mae won't come down on the train when she visits. There are so many trains leaving Boston every day. And when she got to Washington she could travel on the Southern Railway. Where else can you breakfast off real linen tablecloths and heavy silver while you look out at Virginia rolling by? It's a gift, and she ignores it to drive down in that old car."

"Why isn't driving a car as good for you as taking a train?" LeeLee asked, circling Daniel who was himself pacing up and down the platform. "You could always stop and rest along the way. You wouldn't have to drive real fast. Don't you think you could relax doing that, too?"

"This station used to be busy all the time. There were trains that went across the mountains into Tennessee when we first moved here. The most beautiful ride you would want to take, just lovely. But that's gone now. It's a real tragedy." Daniel studied the schedule posted over the station door.

"Danny, you'll make sure you get a calculus class this fall. You won't be acceptable to the good colleges unless you have some more math," Justina said.

"And some European history," Daniel joined in. "You can never study too much history."

"But it's math the colleges will look for. Anybody can read a history book." Nathan, standing on the edge of the platform with his toes sticking over the edge, heard the years of bitterness in his mother's voice, recognized, in his father's refusal to defend himself, more years of indifference. He didn't understand how they ever could have gotten together in the first place.

"You'll have to take North Carolina history this year." LeeLee peered over the edge beside Nathan and drew back with a shudder. "It's required." Eventually she got tired of waiting for him to answer, and went to sit on a bench by herself, pulling a paperback from the pocket of her coat.

Danny stood between his parents like a bony plow horse enduring the flies which tormented his eyes and nose, occasionally tossing his head, bearing with resignation what he couldn't escape. Nathan waited for a wink, a raised eyebrow at Mom's questions, some assurance that all this fuss was as ridiculous as always and that neither family nor school would get in their way: at Christmas they would have six whole weeks to hang out together.

It wasn't a question of talking about love. If Danny had offered some elaborate farewell, saying something like, I love you, kid, Nathan wouldn't have known where to look, what to answer. Thank you? No. What he wanted was, what he had wanted was, to remain with Danny in that easy natural confidence where words weren't important or necessary or even used much, where they moved together anticipating each other's needs like a pair of soccer players passing the ball down the field. Where they both flopped down on the grass at the same time without having to explain to the other that they were tired and wanted a breather. Or moved away from the game altogether, leaving their teammates behind, on the silent signal of one walking off the field.

But there was a gap in that communication, dangerous as a fissure in a stone wall begun by a thin green shoot of ivy whose insistent unseen growth will eventually split the wall apart. That summer Nathan found himself choosing words, shaping sentences, molding questions for his brother in a formal way which made him halt and stumble and finally give up the effort altogether. And he sensed that Danny treated him in the carefully polite way they talked to LeeLee after Mom scolded them for making her cry.

His parents filled in the gaps with questions which Danny answered quietly. He allowed Justina to pull at his collar and dab his cheek with a spit-dampened handkerchief. When the train finally swung around the curve of the track and hissed to a stop, they all got on to watch Danny choose his seat. They stood in a row along the aisle as he swung his suitcase on the overhead rack, taking his suit coat from Justina and, as she watched, spreading it carefully across his bag. Nathan threw the knapsack alongside. Then there was nothing more to do and Danny leaned an arm on the seat back before and behind, stooping a little because of the overhead rack, and listened to final words of advice. LeeLee returned carrying a paper cone full of water, and the news, "There's no one else in the car except an old lady asleep down by the bathroom."

"It'll get crowded at Washington," Daniel predicted. "Well, son, all ashore that's going ashore." He shook hands with Danny. Justina kissed him and hurried down the aisle, only to flutter back with the bag of sandwiches. "Your lunch, I almost forgot to give you your lunch," she said tearfully. Pushed down the aisle and out of the car ahead of his parents, Nathan had time only to give Danny a silent wave which his brother didn't return. As the broad blank back of the train pulled out of reach, his stomach clenched around a painful emptiness. He was left behind with no guarantee that his brother would come back still his brother. He didn't believe that his mother, hands empty now in the pockets of her overcoat, could feel any worse than he did.

Nathan choked on a mouthful of water. He was too far out. He flipped over on his back to rest. He hadn't realized how tired he was. He floated some, swam some, then floated again, slowly nearing the shore. Hannah sat crosslegged on the bank, her head bent. As he got closer, he saw that her hands were working at something in her lap. She greeted him quietly as he pulled himself up beside her.

"You were a long way out."

"Farther than I should have been, I guess." Nathan flopped down on the grass, panting.

"You have to pace yourself and remember that it's always harder coming back than it is going out. Though that's a hard thing to keep in mind on a hot summer day when a lake opens out before you and all you want to do is swim to the end of the world."

Nathan leaned back on his elbows and closed his eyes. Water

rolled off his skin. After awhile the blood in his head quit pounding.

Late afternoon sunlight filtered through the trees, making snakelike shadows of the vines Hannah twisted together into coarse braids. The sky was a weaker blue, as if the long day of heat had diluted its color, leaving it with the milky overcast of an eye with a cataract. To Nathan, the sky seemed as tired as he was of this summer day, Memorial Day, the day that should have signalled the start of glorious summer vacation. But all that lay ahead were long months with only LeeLee for company. Nathan lay flat, his rolled-up jeans for a pillow, one arm partially screening his face from the sun, and stared moodily at the shimmering leaves.

Last summer, Danny ran a lawn mowing service. He took Nathan along on most of the jobs, letting him help mow if the yard wasn't too steep, and clip around the edges of young trees and flower beds. Together they raked the withered grass into long rows, then, their rakes pulling together like oars, made piles of the clippings on the fragrant lawn. Bits of grass would stick to Nathan's sweaty back and arms, causing them to itch unbearably, and his thirst would grow until thoughts of a dripping glass of ice water nearly drove him mad. But they didn't take many breaks. This was business, and the more time they saved by working steadily, the more value the dollar bills counted out to them would have. Danny explained it as sound economics. When one woman fussed that she would have to pay twice as much for two boys, Danny interrupted her. "You don't have to worry about paying him. He's my brother. I take care of that." He draped his arm briefly over Nathan's shoulder.

Her yard was a particularly unpleasant one to work in. She had a steep bank in front which Danny mowed in careful horizontal rows, digging his feet in to keep from slipping down to the road. There were dozens of ornamental weeping cherry trees which had to be clipped around just so. From time to time the woman appeared on her porch, shading her eyes against the sun, peering out at them. Once she yelled at Nathan for neglecting to pull all the weeds from between the terraced steps. Unlike most of their customers, she didn't offer them cokes or iced tea, and they had to rely on the garden hose to keep cool. But Nathan didn't care. As he knelt to trim around the millioneth fruit tree, he was aware only of the companionable roar of the lawn mower which his brother guided. The noise kept them from talking, but it also kept out the rest of the world. All there was was the widening trail of short grass, the hot odor of gasoline, the relief of pulling off a sticky t-shirt and feeling the air dry his back, the knowledge that he was working alongside his brother and that it was like old times.

The noise of the lawn mower was no more barrier to their communication than was the incomprehensible vocabulary Danny had brought home from school. Whenever he talked to Nathan he introduced new names and phrases so casually that it was clear he no longer noticed how strange they were. To Nathan they were exotic, inaccessible, as mysterious as the whiff of incense at Easter Sunday service. Danny talked of "check-in," "proctors," "the grill," as if they were so real they had a smell all their own. Like the words they had grown up with: the cafeteria, which meant not the sumptuous feasts laid out in shopping mall cafeterias but that one particular spot along the junior high hallway just past the bathrooms where the smell of steamed vegetables began, and where the first graders, in order to ensure that the eighth graders ate before 2:45 when the buses started leaving, were halted at 10:30, their long shuffling line curved by irresistible curiosity towards the doors of the older students, while their teacher tiptoed to the glassed-in cafeteria wall to see if they might enter.

Inside were rows of rectangular green-topped tables originally bought for the high school so the younger children ate their lunches with their heads perpetually craning upwards, like baby birds. Each table held six children: once a month, twice, if you were unlucky enough to have a name near the beginning of the alphabet, your teacher sat with you and a fortunate one of your tablemates was sent away to her previous seat. You ate then in miserable silence. No one was supposed to talk at lunch because the cafeteria was built next to classrooms, but at the other, teacherless, tables, mouthed signals grew to murmurs, to explanatory whispers across the table, to discussions as someone else caught a word or two, to arguments that bounced around the cement block walls in great washes of sound, which, on the rebound made answering impossible unless you shouted, and you did, along with the other hundred children, until the sharp and angry crack of Mrs. Peabody's class ring against a table top shut your mouth around the straw in your empty milk carton.

Friday meant a sugar bowl put on each table for the rice served in white gluey mounds that a finger couldn't dent. The students ate off of pale green trays just large enough to hold a pink plastic plate, a yellow dessert bowl, and a milk carton. Exactly 17 minutes after each class had walked through the glass doors, the janitors scraped their leftovers into the special trash barrel so the food could be fed, somewhere down the line, to somebody's hogs. Danny created near-rebellion in the lower grades when he told LeeLee about the state law that said that all those scraps had to be cooked before the hogs were allowed to eat them, and that he was positive he'd seen one of the cafeteria ladies heating them in the great steel soup pot in the school kitchen.

Now Danny talked of his school's dining hall, of drinking coffee there out of white china, of the boys squeezing their chairs together to make room at the table for the headmaster who brought his cup over after dinner and talked to them of his sailboat. Danny spoke as if this were a perfectly normal gesture on the part of a school's head. Nathan, however, smelled the dust which twinkled in the bars of light from the window in front of the principal's office. Mrs. Weber's door was always closed, her secretary's, open, except for the fifteen minutes in the morning when she shut the bottom half to make a counter from which she sold pencils and erasers. If you got there with your money even a minute after 8:15, the shop was already closed and you ran the risk of Mrs. Weber catching you out of a class. "It's past time for prayers!" she would boom. "What are you doing off your hallway?" The voice itself issued from a mouth so obscured by jowls and double chins and the shaking wattles of her upraised arms as she shooed you away that you never dared to look up, and relied on your imagination and the distorted shadow along the floorboards to tell you what she looked like. Danny swore that she was six feet tall. The floor shakes when she's coming, he said matter-of-factly. There's no need for you to ever get caught.

On this judgment, however, Nathan never quite trusted his brother. Something inside would not let him mock the great imperatives which formed the boundaries of behavior. He never learned to cut across to the playground by running past the boiler room, a brick building beneath the school kitchen which stood as a kind of perpetually steamy hell to the lower grades. To go that way meant breaking one of the school's strictest rules: no students allowed in the back lot. It also meant passing the two old janitors who sat there every afternoon, chairs tipped back against the warmth of the brick wall, their blue uniforms unbuttoned down the front to sun the great bellies held in by greyish undershirts. Those were the two who jeered when you passed them in the hall on the way to the bathroom. Nathan would never dare encounter them on their own territory.

He didn't understand how Danny had no awe for the rules, for the teachers who stalked the hallways. To dare go against them invited a sure plunge to disaster: a fiery lecture from Mrs. Weber, at least, and maybe then a whipping, with the threat of several years in a school for delinquent boys where every window was iron-barred and they beat you with bolo paddles. When Danny reached ninth grade, the teachers began calling home to protest his insolence. He got a reputation: "that biggest Pearson boy," and Nathan's teachers began to cast questioning glances at him. Each night Danny would tell Nathan what he'd done that day. School was just a background for his adventures, and Nathan, lying on his side to listen, sometimes forgot that his brother was describing the school they both attended. It was in the middle of that year that Daniel decided his son needed more of a challenge than the local school system could offer. Danny would go to boarding school. He would do well there. He was bright, he was well-liked, he could work when he had to. He always landed on his feet. He could get along anywhere he went. Without a word to Danny, his future was settled.

Nathan waited impatiently for his brother to come back for his first vacation and tell him all about his new life, much as he had always waited for the lights to go out at the end of the day so he could hear the latest of Danny's exploits. But when Danny did come, the house, usually filled with tension, seemed to kindle into open flames. It was too small for them all. Danny paid no attention to the customs they'd grown up with, traditions that ensured Daniel the absolute quiet he demanded to work. Mom scolded constantly; Danny had used the front door when Daniel was asleep on the front porch; Danny had turned on the stereo when he knew his father was typing upstairs. "Your father is working," she hissed, when he pulled Nathan into a wrestling match on the kitchen floor. Her tone picked Nathan right up off the floor and dropped him weak-stomached at the screen door ready to flee. "Working" meant Daniel on the third floor glowering in his office, his hands on the typewriter keys stilled by the noise his boys were making, then his sudden roar down the stairs. "Justina! Can't you keep those boys quiet!" "Sorry, Mom," Danny said casually. "We were trying out a new hold." As if their mother would recognize the importance of their game and allot them as much right to noise as Daniel had to quiet; Nathan disappeared out the door. He never talked to his brother about this. He figured out on his own that what appeared to the grownups as Danny's rudeness was really a new sense of justice and injustice, in which they as children had rights, too. Nathan marvelled that Danny seemed to have forgotten that in their house what mattered were the rules, which stood as if carved in granite. It made him afraid for Danny, that he would ignore those rules. For what certainty was there if he questioned them? Danny was hurrying beyond him, beyond them all, and Nathan could almost hear the cracking of the tree limb as it broke beneath his brother's weight. When they were little, Danny regularly fell from trees; a cast on one arm or the other had been almost a uniform for him. He would climb too far up or move too far out along a branch, often to show Nathan that there was plenty of room for both of them, calling down all the while, It's great! You can see everything! Come on up, there's lots of room!

Often he fell in mid-sentence, and when he recovered his breath from the jolt of hitting the ground, finished what he was saying while he looked up at Nathan who had crouched in terror over his brother's body. Now once again Danny was racing ahead of him to the top of some mysterious tree, his feet confident in infinitesimal toeholds invisible to his brother below, arm muscles pulling him up as gracefully as a dancer, up, up, his head flung back to see where he was going with no thought to what lay below.

Danny, Nathan cried inside, why did you go so far out? There was no sense in stripping off all the past; you had nothing to replace it with. I thought you knew what you were doing. You always did before. If only I had known you had no idea what you were doing, if only I had known you could feel as lost as I do, I would have made you come back. I would have made you come back down.

"If it keeps up as hot as this, it's going to be a hard summer." Hannah had plaited the last of the vines into a wreath and was weaving blue strawlike flowers into the circle. "I think I'll hang it on the front door. Like the Celts hung holly at Christmastime to keep away evil spirits."

"You mean ghosts?" Nathan spoke with an effort past the grief locked in his throat.

"Whatever you want to call them. Whatever it is that wishes you evil instead of good. There." Hannah held the wreath at arm's length to inspect it. "Perhaps this will daunt the neighbors at least. I'm sure that's how many spirits disguise themselves today, as neighbors coming up the road at ten in the morning when you couldn't be anywhere else but home and have no excuse to get rid of them."

Nathan watched as she tucked a flower more securely into place. Her blunt-tipped fingers worked deftly, busy in a world where there was no anxiety, just the steady pulling of vines across one another into a solid form. If he concentrated, perhaps he could remain in her world, without slipping into memory. If he concentrated, he could get by without thinking. At the same time, he recognized that it was the peace emanating from Hannah, that calm around her that gave him hope that he could just be without thought; it was that very stillness that was enabling him to see his family, himself, so clearly. As he could never have done at home.

"There's a book in our school library full of pictures of ghosts and haunted houses," he offered. "They have special cameras now that can take pictures of that kind of thing."

"Do they." Her hands continued to break off flower stems to regular lengths and push them through the wreath. "And what do these spirits look like on paper?"

"Lights." He knew every picture in that book by heart. He had studied them again and again, drawn at first by the terror they roused in him, and then because he was looking at something which was beyond his comprehension. It was like glimpsing, through a bedroom door left partially open, that adult world he was not supposed to know about so that a trembling excitement at his own daring had taken over him. Something inside which had lain dormant was suddenly, furiously awake, and he was alert to things he had never noticed before. He didn't want to lose this new sense. He had forced himself, that old, duller part of himself that was really afraid of the knowledge in that book, to stand before its shelf in the library and take down the book and open to the picture that most disturbed him. At first he had to turn past the page, get several pages between his hand and it; it was too much. A glimpse of its lower corner was enough to conjure up the entire picture, which then haunted him for hours afterwards. His own reason could not convince him that there was nothing to fear. Gradually, he trained himself to look at the page straight on. It was the only American house in the book, some 19th century mansion in New York State. There was a harmless-enough photograph of the entire estate on the previous page; a damp-looking stone house four stories tall, broad-shouldered and rambling, ringed in by several levels of gardens. Then, the picture: a broad stairway which curved as it came down, opening wider at the bottom like a mouth. Gold-framed portraits hung along its left wall, a dark banister curled down the other side. In the center of the picture, just where the stairs began to widen, was a shape caught in blurred movement, coming down. That the shape was blurred was proof to Nathan that it was real; it seemed to him that any photographer could fake a posed still shape, but to catch just that type of blurred light, no. The shape was clear enough to make out a sort of narrow head with a full triangle of a long dress flowing behind. Both head and body were translucent, so the stairs behind continued down and you could tell the sprigged pattern of the carpet through the misty light which was the figure.

And on the next page was absolute proof. Someone had taken a picture just before the shape appeared, for there was the hallway and the stairs and the photographer himself bending before his camera tripod, waiting. No one who put himself inside a book would lie.

"How do you know?" asked Hannah.

"It's a science book, in the non-fiction section. Non-fiction means not made up, the books are about real things. Stories and that kind of stuff are on different shelves."

"And everything these scientists write about is going to be true?" Hannah laid the wreath aside with an admiring pat, and leaned back on her elbows, gazing across the lake.

"Scientists work from facts. They aren't allowed to make up anything. They make observations about what really is. Just like historians; they aren't allowed to make up the past. My dad's a historian. He writes books about what happened in the 18th century, nothing made up. And I'll probably be a scientist so I know how they work."

"Is that right." Hannah didn't offer that automatic voice of praise with which most adults greeted his intention. He was used to answers like, yes, now that's a wonderful field to be interested in, that's where all the important discoveries are being made, that's where the money is. Hannah just stretched her arms to the sky as if blessing it. "Welcome, evening. We need to see you. The cool is coming, Nathan, can you feel it? We ought to celebrate; it's the most beautiful time of the whole day."

She began to pull her socks on without waiting for his answer. Suddenly Nathan felt like a very small boy who has been indulged but not really listened to.

'You sound just like LeeLee," he flung at her. "She thinks science is silly, too. She doesn't even notice what's going on in the world. All she wants to do is read her dumb stories; all she wants to do is escape from what's really happening."

"Not necessarily a bad idea, up to a point." Hannah shuffled her feet into her tennis shoes without bothering to re-tie them. "As long as you touch base with the facts now and then. I certainly don't go so far as to condemn modern science. Perhaps you're reading more into what I said than I meant. That's a dangerous practice to get into, don't you think?"

No, I don't. Nathan glared at the ground. In my family that's how you figure out what's going on, by listening to what's left unsaid.

"If and when you feel like it, you're welcome to come back up to the house. You could take a shower. We could have some supper. Then I could show you the quickest way back to the Park. We're quite close, you know."

She left him, then, though Nathan couldn't believe that she could so casually just walk up the trail without him, without staying to make sure what he was going to do. He took a few steps after her, not completely willing to be left behind. But there was some part of him that would not give in easily, that would not just go along with this old lady's suggestions, and so he refused to put on his sneakers. As if, the rational part of his brain mocked him, that was going to prove anything to Hannah. But they were his feet which curled away from the sharp surprise of roots and small rocks, and when he set his heel on a particularly cruel rock, he stopped, shooting a furious glance at the indifferent pale blue cotton back of the old lady as it vanished around a corner. How dare she walk off and leave him like that. How dare she pretend to give him any kind of advice. She didn't know anything about him. And she didn't know anything about his family.

So what was he going to do now? Hannah was gone, not even a faint rustle of leaves echoing behind her. He was going to sit here and fume about being left alone? Nathan skipped a few rocks across the lake. What would Danny do? That was easy; and Nathan's face relaxed into a smile. When had Danny ever been able to sit beside a body of water bigger than a bathtub without being in it? He didn't have to think about Hannah; he didn't have to think about Aunt Mae or LeeLee or his mother. He didn't have to do anything he didn't want to. All he had to do was get in the water. Nathan folded his glasses and left them on the bank and waded in without a second thought.

He felt cooler at once. His muscles tingled pleasantly, and he struck out for the far shore as confidently as though he could see it. He could swim forever, just like Danny. He was as strong as his brother; he was as daring. He wasn't just the little kid anymore. He was Nathan Pearson, and he could do anything he wanted to do.

But that was crazy. He was caught on every side by people who wanted something from him. He wasn't free. His mother watched every breath he drew these days ,and if she wasn't home to do it, Aunt Mae was lurking behind him with her quiet but still demanding expectations. LeeLee was waiting for him, somehow, to reach in and pull her away from her books. He couldn't stand it. There must be something wrong with him, the way there was something wrong with his family. And now there was even this old lady, this Hannah, waiting for him—he could just hear what his mother would make of Hannah. She would push her freshly-washed hair off her face in that radiant college-girl gesture and stare at Hannah until there was nothing left of her but the category: crazy old lady.

But that wouldn't be fair. Hannah was all right. She was the only one of them who left him a choice, who left him free to think. She didn't hover. She trusted him.

Or maybe it was that she didn't care. He wasn't her responsibility.

Nathan felt suddenly tired, weighted down. Don't go swimming by yourself, Danny cautioned him. Even when you're good. You're just asking for trouble. You can get a cramp just like that; you never know what's going to happen. You need somebody around, in case. Nathan flipped over on his back to rest. He was too far from either shore to glimpse the tops of trees. He couldn't see anything, just the usual depthless grey fog swirling around up where, for most people, the sky would be, with clouds a perceptible distance away. In a panic, he turned back over and began to swim, splashing heavily. He couldn't get his breathing coordinated with his arms and kept gulping water. Every stroke was wearing him out.

Relax. The word came unbidden to his brain. You're fighting the water, kid. It'll hold you up if you let it. Automatically, Nathan rolled onto his back and stretched out, tipping his head until water covered his ears. He felt like Danny's hand was beneath his head, supporting it, the other hand beneath his shoulder blades. He didn't strain to see. When Danny was with him, he didn't worry about distances, but focused on sights immediately beside him: the fin-like wiggle of Danny's foot as he dived beneath the surface, the freckles on his shoulders when he shot out of the water. When, gently, Danny took his hands away, Nathan didn't sink but floated, buoyant, as his brother had promised. He kicked slowly, trusting the water to hold him up, trusting that his body would be held up. You're doing all right, kid. You're doing great. Danny only called him kid when they were feeling close. Nathan raised his head to grin at him. In response, his body sank; hastily he lay back, content to kick towards shore.

It seemed like he had been swimming an awfully long time. He didn't think they had gone this far out. His legs were beginning to tire, and he had to fight the urge to turn and see how much further he had to go.

"Nathan! He couldn't see the shore, much less the body that the voice belonged to, but the sound sent strength surging through his arms and legs and he dared to flop back into the crawl. "Nathan!" The voice seemed to urge him on, and he swam almost gleefully now, undisturbed by the rasping sound as he took in air, some-times breathing in water; he had never been good at the crawl. He switched to breast stroke. Danny didn't know he'd learned it. Effi-cient, arms and legs pulling together in graceful unity, he swam the final yards. The figure on the bank shielded its face with a bent arm. Brown hair gleamed in the late afternoon sun above the crook of the elbow. It crossed Nathan's mind to wonder why Danny hadn't jumped in to help him these last few yards, but the thought flashed through and was gone before it could trouble him, leaving him, instead, with renewed pride that Danny wasn't going to insult him by offering help. Weeds from the lake bottom tickled his knees. He could walk in from here if he wanted to. He had made it.

The figure, in white t-shirt and jeans, reached out to him as he splashed up the bank. "Nathan. I've been so worried about you," said his Aunt Mae.

He couldn't talk to her at first. Silently he towelled off on his t-shirt and pulled on his jeans. They were warm from the sun, rough to skin which had been underwater so long. Aunt Mae had tactfully turned her back to him and was looking over the lake. Nathan shoved his feet into his sneakers and knelt to lace them. His aunt was wearing sandals, flat leather sandals with thin straps. If she didn't have any more sense than to wear shoes like that out here—his deep disappointment, his anger at emotions he couldn't begin to focus, came out as irritation. She had no business being in the woods. She obviously didn't know the first thing about being out here.

"Didn't anybody ever tell you to wear sturdy shoes when you hike? You could step on anything, twist an ankle. What are you doing out here, anyway? Following me?" How could he possibly have mistaken her for Danny? She turned to face him. "Why can't you leave us alone?" he said.

"Nathan," she said. Her voice was beseeching. "I don't know why you won't talk to me. We used to be friends, didn't we?"

"Before you moved in to stay." Into Danny's room. He was too angry to even look at her; he hated the way she looked.

She ignored the deliberate rudeness in his tone. "I'm not moving in to stay. I have a life of my own, you know. I have a career in Boston. I have friends up there."

"You have a boyfriend," he said in a sing-song, mockingly.

"I have a man I care about and who cares about me, yes." She was looking steadily at him; he couldn't stand it. "Someday you'll understand how precious that is, that someone cares about you, and how rare."

"So go back up to him then and leave us alone."

"I can't," she said, and the simplicity of her assertion left him unable to answer back.

"Nathan," she said. "Look at me." Reluctantly he turned his head to face her and, after a moment, let his eyes meet hers. "Nathan, you've been angry and upset since all this happened—"

"All this! All this!" Fury, at her for all the hurt of the past year, at himself for wanting to hurt her, at Danny for hurting him, his fury came into focus with the words "You can't even call it what it is! You're just like the rest of them!" He jerked away from her outstretched hand. "It's not 'all this.' It wasn't a car accident. Danny killed himself and you won't talk about it. You won't even use the words. Danny killed himself." His voice cracked with his tears, and then raged on, high-pitched, panting. "And no one will tell me why he did it. How am I going to find out if he was crazy or not? How am I going to know if I'm crazy?" He clawed at his face to get rid of the tears. "What are you doing out here? Why can't you leave me alone?"

"I'm sorry, Nathan. I'm sorry." The shrill insistent chorus of spring peepers rose around them. Aunt Mae said, "You were gone such a long time. Your mother was worried about you."

"Then she should have come after me. Why do you have to do her dirty work?" he said. He didn't expect an answer, and she didn't give him one. He watched dully as the touch of a fish to the surface of the lake sent a circle rippling outwards. The sun had dropped low in the sky; long shadows from the pines on the far shore slanted across the water. Nathan shivered. It was all out now. His body felt weak and empty.

"Nathan," Aunt Mae was holding him by the shoulders. It wasn't an embrace he could shake off, but the firm grip of strong musician's fingers which dug to the bone. "We need to talk. That's the only reason I've stayed around. To talk to you. LeeLee, she'll be okay. But you—. I've been waiting for the right time. I guess I just have to make the right time," she said as if to herself, and took a deep breath. "I don't know why Danny killed himself. I honestly don't. I've worried and worried over that. And all I can say is that it was for no simple reason. It wasn't just because of pressures at school or because your parents argue or because he was crazy. Yes," and she tightened her grip as he flinched, "I know what Daniel said. You have to remember that he's been hurting, too, and when you hurt you want a clear and simple answer for why something happened. You want somebody, something, to blame. Saying Danny was crazy gives your father something tangible to hang onto, to understand. The way being angry at me has given you something to focus on. But Danny wasn't crazy. He was confused about a lot of things, maybe. Certainly he needed something from us which none of us gave. Reassurance that he was all right, that his life was all right, that it would all straighten out. We failed him. I know I failed him. I was too wrapped up in my own life. Your parents failed him. Maybe you failed him, too."

"He failed us!" Nathan cried.

"He made the wrong choice," she said quietly. She had not yet let go of him, but was working her fingers into his shoulders, kneading, and Nathan felt the strength of her hands willing away the tension, the fear, that had kept him rigid for so many months. He could almost have leaned back against her and accepted her embrace. His resentment of her began to ease away like a muscle cramp which has no good cause.

"If only I had woken up earlier—" he began.

"Your mother has lived her whole life according to 'if only,'" Aunt Mae said. "Don't you start."

"But if he realized when it was too late that he made the wrong choice—"

"Yes," she said.

"So what do I do?" he cried.

Aunt Mae loosened her grip on his shoulders and stood beside him. The lake was absolutely still, waiting for evening. "Do what we all have to do," she said. "Miss Danny. Think about him. But not all the time. Get on with your life."

"And never trust myself or anyone else again," Nathan muttered.

"We were all responsible for Danny," Aunt Mae said slowly. "And we're all guilty of failing him. We can't deny that; it's just something we all must live with from now on. But I wonder—." She sounded as if she were feeling her way with words. "I wonder if every human being on this earth falls short of his responsibility to other human beings. I'm not trying to excuse myself or you. But there's so much we ought to do for one another, and either we don't see, or something in us gets in the way and we don't do. It's so hard to put into words."

"We're selfish," Nathan supplied.

"No. No, it's not that at all. It's just that we're human. We fall short. But we keep on trying."

It wasn't that she was telling him anything particularly profound or stirring. But, Nathan thought, she meant what she said, and more, she was concentrating every ounce of her being on figuring out what to say to him. She was holding nothing back. He could feel that. No part of her, as she spoke, was preoccupied with other thoughts. She talked to him, he realized, the way Hannah listened.

He would be able to say things to her, then, and not worry that she would react from her own worries; he was going to be able to talk about what mattered.

He turned to her. "Do you know the way back?"

She laughed shakily. "More or less."

"We'll try. And if not, I know someone who can show us the way." Nathan started up the bank, then leaned down to give her a hand, for her sandals were slipping and sliding on the dirt. Then side by side they started through the woods towards Hannah's house, towards home.

MARGARET STEPHENS was raised for the most part in Knoxville, Tennessee, where she and her three brothers studied piano and violin from an early age. After graduating from the Phillips Exeter Academy and Harvard University, she returned to East Tennessee to write for *The Knoxville News-Sentinel*. She completed a Master's in English Literature from the University of North Carolina–Chapel Hill while writing *Brother's Keeper, Sister's Child*, and now lives in Sewanee, Tennessee, with her husband and young son.

Brother's Keeper, Sister's Child
was designed and composed at Bull City Studios,
and typeset at Tseng Information Systems, Inc.,
Durham, North Carolina.
Printed at Braun-Brumfield, Inc.,
Ann Arbor, Michigan.

Library of Congress Cataloging-in-Publication Data

Stephens, Margaret, 1958-
    Brother's keeper, sister's child.

    I. Title.
PS3569.T385287B7   1989   813'.54   89-969
ISBN 0-932112-26-9

Cover photo by Ted Bodenheimer

The publication of Brother's Keeper, Sister's Child is made possible, in part, by grants from the North Carolina Arts Council and the National Endowment for the Arts, a federal agency.

BROTHER'S KEEPER, SISTER'S CHILD